"I was looking for an angel . . . and I found one. . . ." So saying, he had her well into his embrace.

She did not know why, but she was not frightened in the least. She released a short laugh and advised him as she pulled away.

"Well, you are wrong, for I am no angel!"

He had her back in his arms and his voice was husky now with the intent of his measure. "Are you not?" This time she didn't have the opportunity to reply for his lips were already on hers. His hand pressed her body against his own and he felt a sudden surge of sure desire.

Also by Claudette Williams:

Regency Romances

SASSY*
JEWELENE
LACEY*
MARY SWEET MARY*
LADY BRANDY
HOTSPUR & TAFFETA
SWEET DISORDER*
LADY MAGIC
LORD WILDFIRE*
REGENCY STAR*
LADY BELL*
LADY MADCAP*

Historical Romances

PASSIONS'S PRIDE
DESERT ROSE . . . ENGLISH MOON*
SONG OF SILKIE*
FIRE AND DESIRE*

*Published by Fawcett Books

CHERRY RIPE

Claudette Williams

FAWCETT CREST · NEW YORK

To my blue-eyed Allah with love

A Fawcett Crest Book
Published by Ballatine Books
Copyright © 1988 by Claudette Williams

Library of Congress Catalog Card Number: 87-91088

ISBN 0-449-21279-3

Manufactured in the United States of America

First Edition: April 1988

"Her eyes like angels watch them still;
  Her brows like bended bows do stand,
  Threatening with piercing frowns to kill
  All that attempt with eye or hand
  Those sacred cherries to come nigh,
  Till 'Cherry-ripe' themselves do cry."

THOMAS CAMPION

Chapter One

Lord Drummond stood at his bow window, the cozy warmth of his richly appointed study at his broad back. Before his deep blue eyes was the quiet London street. His right hand had formed a fist at his sensuous lips, for he was in deep concentration. His left hand rubbed his muscular thigh unconsciously. It was a movement born of agitation. The time had come to make his decision final. He would wed, and his bride would be Miss Shauna Elton.

It was his only logical choice. At least one could not fault her heritage, her upbringing, her family connections. Hers was a fine aristocratic line. Her father had been in politics; he had been a Whig like himself, and this was a plus. Miss Elton was reputed to be a lovely creature, though he had heard some talk about her high spirits. No matter; if this was so, he could easily bring her in tow with their marriage. Her age was one and twenty, so he was not robbing the cradle. It was a good age, beyond schoolgirl notions, old enough to mother his brothers and sisters. He had been told that she had a good head on her shoulders, which was well, for she would need it when she found herself with such a large ready-made family.

There, too, Miss Elton had lost her father some years ago. She would understand what it was to lose one's parents, having lost both herself. She knew what it was to be raised by a stepmother and perhaps would use that knowledge wisely when presented with his young brood of siblings. That was in her favor. There it was. Though he had never met her, he had quite made up his mind to it. She would be the one to carry his name!

He turned away from the window and moved toward his Regency writing desk. There sat an impressive grouping of miniatures. One was a portrait of his late mother. On either side of her was a framed portrait of a man. His father, and his stepfather. Then, in order of their age, were the miniatures of his two half brothers and two half sisters. There was Freddy, seventeen and away at Eton. There was Mary, fourteen and also away at school. Then there were the twins, Felix and Francine. The twins were eight years old and totally wild. They had managed to dispose of one governess after another, three in one year. Damn, but they needed a woman's hand. Indeed, he had made the right decision. Marry he would, and his bride would be Shauna Elton!

Lady Elton had become decidedly plump during her years of mourning her deceased husband. Theirs had been a marriage of fifteen pleasant years, for they had been friends, good friends. Lines were etched into her face that had not been there two years before, and she sighed over the fact as she gazed into her hand mirror.

"Ah well," she said out loud. She had never been a pretty woman, and then again out loud, "No matter." She was nearing five and fifty; she had married late in life and did not expect to walk that particular route again. She looked up as a knock sounded at her bedroom door, and her brow went up. Here was her stepdaughter at last!

Lady Elton had been awaiting the child for more than an hour. Child? Certainly past that, though Shauna's behavior was little more than that of a child. She had been allowed to run wild for too long, but she was such a taking

2

little thing that it was hard to curb her. This time, however, she had gone too far. "Come in," she called sternly, and braced herself. Shauna had a way of looking at her that nearly always softened her resolve. Childless herself, she had taken Shauna as her own.

The door opened a trifle, and a black-haired, gray-eyed imp of a girl peeped round and smiled sheepishly. "You wanted to see me, Mama?"

Lady Elton's expression was grave and her voice reproving. "Indeed." She indicated the lady's yellow satin chair near her with an inclination of her head.

Shauna closed the door at her back and went to take up her place with uncharacteristic meekness. Sweetly she folded her hands in her lap and studied her slender fingers. She knew she was in for it. She knew, for she was aware that her latest escapade had caused something of a stir amongst the beau monde.

"Shauna . . . I want you to listen to what I have to say before you get yourself in a state—" started Lady Elton.

"Mama . . . I know now that what I did was not quite the thing. . . ." interrupted Shauna, raising her lashes just a trifle before her gaze immediately dropped to her lap once more. Oh-oh, her stepmother was in no mood!

"Not quite the thing!" Lady Elton spluttered. "Hopping on Lord Melville's stallion in the middle of Hyde Park . . . in your walking clothes . . . riding the animal astride . . . racing Sir Peter . . . for all the world to see . . . not quite the thing? Why, you miserable wretch of a girl! How can you sit there and look the innocent?"

Shauna felt her temper tickle her spine, and she raised not quite meek gray eyes to her stepmother's face. "Had I been a man and done that, I would have been called a top sawyer . . . but because I am a female—"

"Enough! You know the rules that govern society. You know that what you do affects not only your own standing, but mine as well. How dare you, child!"

This tore at Shauna, for she loved her stepmother and meant her no trouble. It was so very difficult.

"Mama . . . I didn't think of that . . . all I know is that . . . Peter was being the very devil of a tease . . . and there was Melville's black looking so very fine and inviting . . . and Melville goading me to ride him. . . ."

"Impulsive creature. It will not do." Lady Elton shook her head. "Never mind. He still wants you. He knows about your latest folly, and the amazing thing is that he still wants you. Says what you need is an outlet . . . and seems to think his—"

"What *are* you talking about?" asked Shauna, puzzled, "Who wants me?"

"I knew that he was interested, but I never dreamed he would actually come up to scratch. . . . And then Lady Jersey said you would be refused vouchers to Almack's because of your hoydenish behavior, and I thought my heart would nearly break—"

"Jersey said she would refuse me entrée to Almack's?" Shauna was astounded, for the Jersey rather liked her.

"No, no . . . not Sarah but the other. . ."

"Princess Esterhazy? Stiff-rumped—" started Shauna.

"And that is another thing! Your language. You spout terms like any man. . . . and you must not. Stiff-rumped indeed!"

"Well, I don't care about Almack's anyway," said Shauna with a pout and looking very much like a child.

"Good, for you shan't be admitted there this season, you dreadful girl. However, all is not lost. You will be married . . . to the catch of the century, and they just might change their minds about you yet. No matter, you will be busy enough this season with your new life."

"Married?" Shauna jumped to her feet. "I am *not* going to be married. What are you talking about?" She immediately racked her brain for an answer to this. Had she indicated any partiality for any of her suitors? No. No she

4

had not. What was her stepmama talking about? What absurdity was this? She had refused no less than five offers in the past eight months. It must be someone she didn't even know! Who could have applied to her stepmama without her knowledge?

"You are going to be married, my dear, and one day you shall thank me for taking this high-handed method of settling you comfortably just when you were on the brink of scandal."

"Mama, I don't know what you are talking about, but I will tell you that I have no intention of marrying where my heart is not in it, and my heart is quite intact!"

"You are going to be married, my darling, and he is just the man to set you to rights," said Lady Elton gently, but firmly.

"The devil you say!" returned her wayward stepdaughter in just the style her stepmama deplored.

"Now that is precisely what I mean," sighed Lady Elton. "You cannot go about using expressions like that one. It is most unbecoming."

"And it is not becoming to marry a man I have never seen!" Shauna was near to screaming. Her mama was talking absurdities, and she found it all incredible.

"His lordship is an exceptional man. He is handsome, he is wealthy beyond imagination, with a family name that dates back to—"

"What do I care for that? Mama . . . you are asking me to marry a man I have never met!" screeched Shauna, who was now pacing frantically.

"Yes, dear, but you shall meet him. Shauna . . . I rather think you will like him. He is most charming . . . and has experience enough to—"

"Ah!" accused Shauna. "No doubt he is ancient!"

"Not quite ancient." Lady Elton's tone was dry. "Eight and twenty, and you, my dear, are one and twenty. You are past your first bloom and still on the town. Most odd . . ."

"Odd? It is what I want. I am very willing to remain single forever," retorted Shauna caustically. "Mama . . . this is all ridiculous!"

"No, Shauna, it is not. I don't know exactly what prompted him to offer for you, for quite honestly, he has never seen you either . . . but offer he has, and I have accepted."

Shauna's mouth dropped, and it took a moment for her to recoup for the attack. "Indeed!"

"Shauna . . . do come down from your high ropes," said Lady Elton soothingly. "Some of the best marriages are created in this fashion."

"And some of the worst! Marriage of convenience? For *me*? Never, mama . . . never."

"No? Well, I am afraid you are out there, my love. His lordship will be by in the morning to present himself to you. . . . And Shauna, mark me, you *will* marry him."

"No." Shauna paced. "I won't. . . . This is monstrous of you. . . ."

"I know you think that, but darling, it is not what you imagine. He will treat you with respect. . . . He is wise enough to handle you gently. . . . Why, you will hunt with him in the North, where he has a hunting box; you will—"

"Mama!" Shauna interrupted sharply. "I can't believe you are doing this to me. You have always stood my friend. Now . . . now you are a stranger. . . . Worse, you are nothing more than a . . . a stepmother from some horrid fairy tale!" With which Shauna fled the room.

Chapter Two

Getting out of London was not as easy as Shauna had anticipated. There had been several setbacks, none of which had taken place as she stole out of the house. This had gone off smoothly—too smoothly, for she had breathed a sigh of relief after exiting through the rear door and immediately assumed a far too cocky frame of mind.

She had reached the stables where her stepmother kept their horses and was met by a sleepy groom who eyed her with a touch of disapproval.

"Lookee . . . why . . . it's Miss Shauna. . . !" he ejaculated in some surprise. His gray-brown brows dove and he pulled at his lower lip. "Whot is it, miss . . . trouble?"

"In a manner of speaking . . . I need my horse . . . as quickly as you can . . . and quietly, John . . . please," she whispered, hoping he would not create any more of a stir than he had already done. She could see another stable-hand moving out of the recesses of the barn.

"Now . . . whot can ye be at?" He shook his head. "Her ladyship wouldn't loike ye rambling about on yer horse at night, miss, no she wouldn't. She would 'ave me 'ead, she would, if oi was to saddle yer Bessy and let ye go. . . ."

"Right then. Never mind. I'll saddle Bessy up myself. . . ." said Shauna, quite willing to be reasonable.

He shook his head, for this did not make any sense to him. Thing was, he could see trouble ahead. "She'll 'ave me run through, she will, and nobbut could blame 'er. Oi jest can't let ye go off at this time of night, Miss Shauna. . . ." He was pleading now.

"Can't you?" Shauna's brow was up. "How do you mean to stop me?" She was already moving toward the tack room. He followed her hurriedly, and his voice had changed to a whine.

"Aw now . . . 'ave pity, do. Whot is it? Do ye want me turned off?"

Shauna turned from her saddle and eyed him. "John, you have been with us too long. My stepmother would never do that. . . . And besides, she knows me; she will understand that you are not to blame in this." She took her saddle and bridle over her arms and moved once more toward her horse's stall. She put them down on the saddle rack in the aisle and took up a well-used pad, slung it over her mare's withers, and proceeded to tack her up. John gawked when he realized she had not even taken her lady's saddle.

"Never say ye mean to ride astride . . . in London. . . ?"

"Who is to know? I will have my hood slung low over my head, no one will know me, and then I shall be much more comfortable when I get out of the city." She smiled at him. "Don't fret it, John; I know what I am doing."

"Do ye indeed!" he snapped. "Oi've 'eard ye say that to me countless times and land yerself in the pudding!"

She laughed, "Well, here is hoping that I shan't land myself in the pudding." She tightened the girth, adjusted the noseband, and said with a sigh, "Never mind, John. You will tell my stepmother in the morning, for she shan't notice that I am gone until then, that I simply took my

8

horse and left before you could do anything about it. You had no choice in the matter, so you can't be blamed.''

"Oi can't let it go loike that, Miss Shauna. . . . Oi've got to go to the 'ouse now and tell her ladyship that you've taken off alone. . . . 'Tis me duty." He was shaking his head sadly.

Shauna reached out and touched his shoulder. "Of course, John. You may do just that." So saying, she led her horse to the mounting block outdoors and hoisted herself into the saddle. She smiled to herself, for her ladyship had gone off to the theatre with friends more than an hour ago. They wouldn't know that in the stable because her ladyship had been taken up in her friend's carriage. This was perfect. She turned and smiled. "Don't worry, John. I have my little pistol with me, plenty of the ready, and I shall do just fine. You may tell my stepmother that I shall write her after I am established and have forgiven her. . . ." Her voice trailed off on this last. Forgiven her? Could she ever forgive her? She had actually promised to marry her off to someone unknown. This was beyond forgiveness . . . or understanding!

Lord Drummond gave his present situation a great deal of serious contemplation and concluded that he was a young man greatly to be pitied. Depression weighed him down until there was only one thing that he could do: drink himself into oblivion! Well, he reasoned with his better sense, he *was* sacrificing his life, wasn't he? He was being totally unselfish and giving the remainder of his life over to a strange woman for the sake of his family. Egad! He would soon be a husband, perhaps a father. All joy would soon be out of his reach . . . gone forever. . . .

Damnation. Life in fact, as he had known it, was certainly quite at an end. There was nothing for it; he would go to his friends, and they would all become royally inebriated together. This decision was taken on with great

9

zeal and enthusiasm as his intimates toasted him and the end of his bachelorhood at White's.

Usually Damien Drummond found that he could drink most men under the table before he began to show signs of being foxed. He was, however, at this stage when he rose suddenly from the table, called for his coach to be sent for, and announced his intention of departing the club for home.

"What's that you say?" Sir James attempted to sit up, for he had been resting his head on his bent arm, which was laid on the card table. "You leaving, Damien. . . ?"

"Must, Jimmy-boy. Have to present myself to my future bride in the morning. Don't want to scare the chit with bloodshot eyes and a haggard face. . . ."

Sir James grinned. "Too late, love!" He slid back against his chair and surveyed his closest friend through half-closed lids. "Don't do this, Damien. . . . You're not ready. . . ."

His lordship's hand found Sir James's gold silky hair and ruffled it affectionately. " 'Tis done already. . . . Never mind, you will be following my lead soon enough, and then we will muddle through marriage together."

"Blister it, man! Damn if ever I will marry!" retorted Jimmy caustically.

His lordship laughed, bade everyone good-night, and made his way outdoors. His driver and coach stood waiting, but he signalled his intention to walk, for he wanted the night air to clear his head. There was a strong, cool breeze, but it in no way cleared the fog he was walking unsteadily through. This was in part ascribable to the very excellent brandy he had managed to imbibe and to the fact that a heavy fog had indeed descended upon London. He turned a corner, frowning over the fact that he could scarcely see more than ten feet in front of him, when something startled him into a sharp, uncharacteristically awkward movement!

Shauna was not in the habit of riding her horse hard on the pavement, let alone on a dimly lit street; however, circumstances warranted speed. She had no doubts as she slowly worked her mare toward freedom. She was doing the correct thing. She would not be forced like some meek nothing of a girl into a loveless marriage! Such thoughts kept her temper in the boughs, and thus she did not think of the dangers of her expedition. A fog had moved in, she made an incorrect turn, backtracked, and found herself suddenly surrounded by a group of young, grimy street urchins. They blocked her path, and she put on a dark look as she commanded, "Do stand aside." Her tone was firm and showed no signs of the sudden panic that she was beginning to feel.

"Whot's this. . . ? A mort, God love ye! A blooming mort . . . Fancy, ain't she?" said one of them, and he moved closer.

Shauna lifted her crop. "I wouldn't come any nearer if I were you. I wouldn't like it." There was a threat in her voice, in the style of her movement.

He looked at the four boys spreading round Shauna and her mare and snorted, "She wouldn't loike it, lads. . . . Whot say ye to that?"

Shauna didn't wait for their answer. She cropped Bessy into a canter and headed straight for the boy. He cursed out loud and jumped out of her way. She rounded the bend in the street, and there Bessy could stand no more. The poor mare found something dark weaving toward her and, with a snort, hopped a rear. Shauna released a short cry, for she wasn't ready, and then grabbed at her horse's neck as she attempted to keep her seat. Bessy shied to the left, and this force of movement sent Shauna the remainder of the way to the ground. She landed on her feet, but lost her balance and reeled backward into a body that felt more like iron than man!

His lordship found his hat was sent spinning as he received a neat bundle thudding into his chest. This was an unexpected assault, and he held to the attacker as he attempted to evaluate the situation. Shauna saw that her mare was looking frightened and ready to run, so she pulled hard to yank herself out of his steel grip. "Let me go . . . do . . . please, I have to catch Bess!"

The appeal in her voice brought his eyes to her face, and he found himself raising a brow. Here was a beauty! He took over.

"Stay here!" He turned and moved gently, and amazingly in control of his limbs, as he went toward the mare and reached for her reins. He could see the whites of her eyes, and she put her nose up and away; however, she made no attempt to run. He took up the reins and then led her towards Shauna.

"Your horse," he said softly.

"Thank you, but you didn't have to. . . . I could have gotten her," returned Shauna, feeling suddenly shy. Here was this fashionable, handsome rogue, and she looked a fool.

"Ungrateful girl, and after you nearly knocked me down," he teased. His speech was only slightly slurred, but enough for Shauna to raise a brow and regard him with some amusement.

"But I did not, and you, sir, were the cause of it all!" she returned, a smile curving her lip. "Whatever were you doing walking about in the middle of the road?" It was a counterattack to save face.

"I? Well, I was looking for an angel . . . and I found one. . . ." So saying, he had her well into his embrace, regardless of the fact that the driver of his coach watched with some keen interest at his back.

She did not know why, but she was not frightened in the least. She released a short laugh and advised him as she pulled away, "Well, you are wrong, for *I* am no angel!"

He had her back in his arms, and his voice was husky now with the intent of his measure. "Are you not?" This time she didn't have the opportunity to reply, for his lips were already on hers, already parting. His tongue found its way easily and teased with gentleness. His hand pressed her body against his own, and he felt a sudden surge of sure desire.

Shauna was astonished, as much at herself and her reaction as she was at his sudden move. She was certainly a virgin, but she had been kissed before, and the fact that this stranger's kiss aroused her as no other's ever had was something of a shock. That frightened her, for she didn't like the notion that she was losing control. She slapped at his shoulder, and when he released her to look into her clear gray eyes, she frowned at him and announced in a whisper, "You, sir, are taking a liberty. I am at a loss, for you are taller, stronger, and perhaps wicked enough to pursue this further. If that is what you intend . . . proceed, for I have always wondered what it would be like to be ravished on a London street." This was meant to make a mark, and it did that very well.

He pulled himself up to his full six feet and stared hard at her. "My dearest child, I am not in the habit of ravishing young women on London streets."

"Ah, then I do apologize," she said meekly. Again a flush hit.

He nearly growled at her, "What the bloody hell are you doing out here alone anyway? 'Tis folly." He was, he thought, fast sobering up.

"Running away from my stepmother. Don't ask why, I shan't tell you, but it would be very nice if you let me go on my way before I am caught," returned Shauna, smiling charmingly at him.

For no reason at all he found himself curious. "Running

13

away? Stepmother? This sounds like some blasted fairy tale. Can't go about London alone at night. Might be accosted by any number of scalawags.''

''So you have made me aware. . . .'' she started.

He took up her arm. ''I shall take you to where you are going.'' He was not the least bit sober.

''But I am going to the New Forest,'' she returned.

''Are you? Whatever the hell for?'' he asked, his brow well up.

''My nanny lives there. She will know what to do.''

''For no good reason, that makes sense. Take you to your nanny,'' announced his lordship.

Chapter Three

Shauna peered through the dim light of the coach at her companion and wondered how it was she had allowed him to take her up in his coach. She knew nothing about him. Yes, but he was such a splendid figure of a man. He was quite thoroughly drunk. Yes, but he held himself in excellent style. He had stolen a kiss. Yes, but such a kiss! She relaxed against the luxuriant squabs of the seat and contemplated the dark scenes slowly passing, for he had evidently gone to sleep.

He was not asleep, but watching her thoughtfully from eyes only half-closed. She was certainly a beauty, he thought after surveying the flitting expressions of her lovely countenance. There was something of the child in her and a sure promise of a woman, perhaps a passionate woman. The notion stirred his desire, but still he reclined.

She grew warm and slipped off her cloak, setting it to one side of herself. She wore a simple, but fashionable, traveling spencer of forest green with black frogging, and she undid the large black buttons of the spencer to reveal a sheer white lace shirtfront. She was unaware of his lordship's interested gaze, unaware of the heat she was causing him to feel, until he sat up suddenly and inquired in a husky voice, "Well then . . . a name. I must have a name."

"Oh." It was very nearly a gasp, for he had startled her. "I thought you were asleep."

He moved to her side of the coach and pressed close. "Now, how could I sleep with you so near?"

"Hmmm," she returned ageeably, "I had been thinking the same about you."

He laughed and looked at her closely before he took up her gloved fingers, found her wrist, and put it to his lips. "Now then, my love, what is your name?"

She had been searching her mind for a name. She chose her nanny's surname but still only gave him her first. "Shauna."

He smiled. "Lovely, but is it not followed by another?"

"Corbett," she answered without meeting his eyes, and before he could pursue this line, she put in her own question. "And yours, sir?"

"Ah, shall I tell you . . . now, or later?" He was nibbling behind her ear.

His efforts sent bolts of pleasure through her, but she controlled the sensation and pulled away. "Now, if you please," she answered. "And do stop that, sir."

It irritated him that she called him sir. It was not what he wanted to hear. "Damien," he said softly. "My name is Damien."

She smiled. "And is it not followed by another?"

He was reluctant to tell her that he was Lord Drummond. It might put her to caution, it might make her feel uncomfortable, and it could get him into trouble. "All you need to know is Damien."

"Is it? And will you take heed if Damien is all I have to call you by?"

"If your lips speak, I must always take heed," he answered gallantly.

She giggled, "Then do release me, sir, for you have me in quite a tight grip."

Indeed, he had her pressed to himself, but he smiled

and answered, only loosening his hold a mite, "You still have not called me by my name." Now he bent to drop a kiss upon her lips.

She allowed it for the moment and then said softly, "Damien, please . . . do not. I trusted you not to take unfair advantage of me. . . ."

Her words nearly sobered him and he sat upright, saying lightly, "Advantage is not something I meant to take from you, child. You have naught to fear from me."

She smiled. "Do you see any fear in my eyes?"

He looked into them and said, his voice husky once more, "No, I see warmth . . . and an invitation. Do they lie?"

"No, for you were very kind to take me up and all the way to Lymington. It is a four-hour journey, and the truth is, I was loath to do it by myself in the dead of night."

"Zounds, woman! Don't know what can have driven you to it," he ejaculated with some feeling. There was something kittenish about the chit that was most appealing, and the thought of her alone and subject to the dangers of the night for hours on end was unthinkable.

"I have my reasons, believe me," she answered simply, and smiled softly at him.

"How old are you?" he asked suddenly frowning at her.

"One and twenty . . . or nearly so," she answered truthfully.

"Lord, then why aren't you safely married?" he asked in some surprise.

"Haven't fallen in love yet."

He laughed caustically, "Love don't exist. Settle for comfort."

She sighed, "You are so . . . unfeeling . . . unromantic. I am afraid that I would not *be* comfortable without love in my marriage."

"You don't know what you are talking about. Love is a

17

deuced nuisance. Muck up a person's mind, be sure of it," he grumbled, and sat back against the thick leather squab to contemplate his remark with more anger than sadness.

Shauna stared at him with wide gray eyes and decided, "Oh, I see, some woman has hurt you very desperately."

He scoffed, "Makes a nice tale, but I have never let a woman close enough to hurt me."

"How sad," she returned pugnaciously.

He eyed her. "How sad? For the women who have missed the chance?"

She laughed, "No, silly, that is not what I meant."

"What did you mean, then?"

"I meant that you have a very cynical attitude about women, about love, and that is sad."

"Is it? I rather think it is wise. Love often spoils what a man and woman could have."

"And what can they have without love?" she was surprised into asking.

He answered her in his fashion, with action. Once more she felt herself drawn into his embrace, once more she heard his low murmur, "Here, sweets, let me show you. . . ." as his lips parted hers, nibbled at her lower lip, seduced her tongue until it touched his own.

She drew away from him. He allowed her to do so. She eyed him warily and rebuked gently, "Please, Damien . . . do not."

"No? Don't you want me to kiss you?" he teased, flicking her nose with his forefinger in an easy, affectionate manner.

"Yes, as a matter of fact. You do it so well, and you are so very handsome, that it would be very odd in me not to want you to kiss me; however, I cannot allow it."

He laughed and took up her chin. "I like you, Shauna Corbett." He then sighed, "But you are certainly a brat."

She put up her chin with some hauteur and retorted sharply, "I am too old to be called a brat!"

"Yes, so you are, and you are also too old to be single. You should be married," he returned testily.

She eyed him mischievously then. "Is this a proposal, Damien? You know, just because you have taken a kiss or two, I don't expect you to marry me."

He laughed at that and pulled her back into his arms. "Ay, my beauty, I would need more than a kiss or two. . . ." with which he proceeded to take yet another.

Chapter Four

The morning came blasting before Lady Elton's hazel eyes. It was not the brightness of the day that sent her bolt upright in her bed. It was not the hot cocoa that brought her round and sent her into a tither. It was the answer to the casual question she had put to her mind, "Is Shauna still in bed?"

"No, m'lady . . ." returned the elderly lady's maid warily. She was ready. She feared the worst and had already sent a lackey to the stables to inquire after Miss Shauna, for she had anticipated her lady's next question.

"No? Where is she then?" asked Lady Elton, sitting up and feeling a twinge of something she could not then explain to herself.

"I am not certain, m'lady," returned the maid, avoiding her lady's inquiring gaze.

"Are you not?" Lady Elton's brow was up. She was aware that her dear Maria was fond of Shauna and would "cover up" for her if she could. "Indeed! Have Miss Shauna attend me at once."

"That I would, m'lady, if I could," answered Maria primly, her hands folding into themselves against her midriff.

"But you can't, can you?" Lady Elton was near to shrieking. "Why not? Where has that dreadful girl gone?"

A soft knock sounded at the closed door and Maria went to open it a crack, stepping out into the hall where she could be heard exchanging excited whispers with the young lackey there.

She eyed the boy after he had disclosed all he knew, and then with a wagging finger she warned, "You are not to speak of this. You are to forget anything you have heard. Miss Shauna is in bed with . . . with a quinsy. Do you understand, lad?"

"Ay . . ." whispered the boy, who did not believe for a moment that Miss Shauna was in her room. He, too, knew his mistress, and was fond of her enough to keep the secret.

Maria sized him up with her glance, decided it was safe enough, and sent him off to finish his work. She braced herself and turned to reenter her ladyship's bedchamber. There she found Lady Elton up and pacing.

"Well?" Lady Elton was already in a state.

"It would appear that Miss Shauna has . . . run away. . . ." Maria was close to tears. To think of her pet off by herself, God only knew where . . . well, it did not bear thinking.

"Run away?" Lady Elton sank into the blue satin winged chair near her fireplace. "Run away. . . ?"

"Ay! The poor wee darlin'. Ye can't go bringing a lass like that to her knees! It won't fadge, and so I told ye. . . ." Maria's tongue had lapsed into her natural dialect.

"Run away? But . . . why. . . ?"

"M'lady." Maria clucked her tongue and shook her head. "Need ye be asking? Did ye not tell her she had to marry a man she had never clapped eyes on?"

"Faith! What shall I tell him? Maria! He will be here at ten o'clock this morning, and what shall I tell him?"

"Miss Shauna won't be seeing callers! She is in bed with a quinsy."

"A quinsy. Of course. A quinsy. It will give us time. No doubt the dreadful brat has gone off to one of her friends and will be back presently."

"Do ye think so, m'lady?" asked Maria doubtfully.

"What else can I think?" Lady Elton felt a wave of sickness shake her inner being. "My girl has always been so capable, so clever. . . . Maria . . . she must be safe. . . ." A tear formed and rolled down her white cheek. "Maria . . . I would not have made her marry his lordship if she had taken him in dislike. It was just that I thought if she saw him . . . He is so very handsome, just in her style. . . . Well, I thought they would take—"

"Shauna is not a biddable girl, m'lady. Ye set her against him just by telling her she hadn't a choice."

"Oh, faith . . . faith . . . I see that now. . . ." Lady Elton put her hand to her forehead. "What shall I do. . .?"

"We give her the day, m'lady . . . don't ye think? She is a good-hearted girl. Won't want to think of you distressed. She will come back. . . ." Maria thought about this and had her doubts. Shauna in a temper might not see that Lady Elton would be distressed.

"Yes, yes. She is the most compassionate creature. She will come back today. . . ." and then because Lady Elton remembered the look on Shauna's face when Shauna realized her stepmother meant her to marry an unknown gentleman, "Oh . . . dear, Maria . . . what if she doesn't? What if she is in trouble?"

"Trouble? Miss Shauna is more likely to be causing it. Don't ye fret now . . ." Maria assured her ladyship, though she, too, was concerned, "Miss Shauna will take care of herself!"

His lordship held his head, closed his eyes against the morning sun's strong rays, and groaned. He had to steady himself. He reopened his eyes and found his reflection in the long looking glass before him. "Egad!" he breathed out loud, and groaned again.

He looked the very devil. His blue eyes were bloodshot. His black hair was ruffled in wild disorder, and he looked older than his years. Last night had become something of a blur. How he had made it home, how he had made it to his bed, was a total mystery, for he could not recall these particular details.

What he did recall, vividly, was a pair of sparkling gray eyes and a lilting, musical bubble of a laugh. Little vixen. Somehow she had dragged him to the New Forest itself . . . or had he offered to escort her there? No matter, there was where he had found himself, waking up a plump and elderly woman who clucked her tongue at both of them and ushered them within. He smiled. There was something unreal about the memory. Had she been so lovely, so desirable? Why had he let her get away without bedding her? What had happened?

It was that woman! That's right, he remembered now. The Corbett woman. She had made him take tea . . . by the fire, and there had been something pleasant about it all. He shook off the memory with a touch of irritation. He was being maudlin. Damnation to bloody hell! He was about to meet his future wife. What was he doing? Yet . . . there was her kiss. He could taste it still. Shauna Corbett, eh? He had put Polly Corbett in his head as a retired governess and Shauna (as they carried the same surname) some relative of sorts. There was a mystery there, for the little vixen had the look, the air of quality. Just why should she run off to the New Forest in the dead of night? And why should he be bothering his head about it now?

Time was he called his man to aid him with his clothes, for the hour was drawing near. He would have to present himself to his bride. Life would soon settle into genteel, predictable, and perhaps happy married life. Perhaps?

What if she turned out to be a shrew? What if she turned out to have a grating laugh . . . a snide lip . . . a . . . zounds! Life could turn out to be hell! No. He was master of himself, his fate, and he would be master of his wife. He would tame whatever shrew appeared in her, and he would walk away from a grating laugh. Damn, he would teach her from the start what he expected in a wife! And Shauna would be just another memory, neatly put aside.

The sun's morning rays were brighter still in the New Forest. Shauna blinked, moved lazily in her soft bed, and then, with sudden recall, sat bolt upright. "Faith!" she exclaimed out loud as the events of the night came pouring into her mind. She had slept like a baby. She couldn't even remember dreaming. Now, in the newness of the morning, she realized just what she had done. "Oh . . . faith . . ." She breathed the words and her eyes rose heavenward. "What have I done?"

In the night, in her rage, in the impulse of the moment, it had seemed her only recourse. Was she wrong? And then she recalled how grave, how firm, how unbending her stepmother had been. In another hour . . . at ten o'clock she would have been greeting a total stranger in the Elton morning room, and that total stranger was supposed to be her future husband! Again she felt a wave of rage, and her doubts fled. She had done the right, the only thing she could do. Her stepmother had meant business, and well, so did she!

A knock sounded at her bedroom door, and a plump, pink, sweet face appeared. "Ah, so, my little widgeon, you are awake?" said Polly Corbett as she clucked her way into the room and moved to the nightstand to set down her tray.

"Oh Polly . . . Polly, don't be angry. . . ." Shauna was on her feet and throwing her arms around the plump woman.

"Whist with you, silly goose. Of course I am not angry." She sat down on the dark maroon upholstered wing chair and indicated the cup of hot chocolate on the tray. "Now, sip your chocolate and we'll have a nice long chat."

Shauna took up the warm brew, plopped on the bed, and said, "I don't know where to begin . . . and don't tell me at the beginning . . . for then this might take forever. . . ."

"Straight then . . . now, no bends. Start at where you think this particular beginning might be, and if I think there is more . . . I will tell you." Polly Corbett was no fool.

"Well, . . . then perhaps I should tell you that I . . . I have been kicking up something of a lark in London. . . ."

"So I gathered from your letters. . . ." Polly nodded.

"Yes, well . . . my last little adventure . . . seemed to cause more of a stir than my others. . . ." Shauna bit her lip. "Oh, Polly, Mama said that an Almack's patroness had actually indicated to her that I would be refused a season's voucher." She frowned. "Not that I care a fig for such things . . . but Mama does, and I must admit . . . I did find myself snubbed by some of the dowagers." She bit her lip over the problem, sighed, and looked her former governess in the eye. "You would not have approved."

"No, child," said Polly gently, "but tell me before you tell me anything else. What prompted you to create such a fuss?"

"Polly . . . rules . . . rules . . . they are suffocating me in London. I was so used to running at will at Elton Grange. . . ."

"Don't you like London life?" Polly stuck in seemingly on a casual note.

"Yes . . . no . . . it is just that . . . I want to have fun . . . and girls must not do so. We must sit properly, ride properly, converse properly, laugh softly, be stupid . . . or at least not as smart as men . . . and we must marry well!''

''You used to talk of going to London and doing all those things,'' Polly said, and watched Shauna's gray eyes light up with spirit.

''Yes . . . but I also talked of a prince in shining armor . . . doing all the courageous things and saying all the romantic things. Polly . . . there are only rakes or silly boys. . . .''

''So you have been unhappy?''

''I have been . . . disappointed . . . and more recently . . . bored,'' returned Shauna.

''So you took your horse and did what?'' Polly asked knowingly.

''Well, it was with a horse . . . but not with mine!'' Shauna laughed.

''No doubt you galloped through Hyde Park at the fashionable hour,'' said Polly with a shake of her head.

Sheepishly Shauna peeped at her, ''Worse than that.''

''Dear God, there is little that is worse than that!'' returned Miss Corbett in shocked accents.

''I raced this . . . outrageous London . . . beau. . . . Oh, Polly, Mama was so enraged. I have never seen her like that before.''

''Shauna. Never say you ran away because your mama was angry with you.''

''No . . . not exactly . . .''

''And don't try to bamboozle me with a tale about being shy of gossip. You have never given a fig for such things.''

''No . . . not exactly . . .'' repeated Shauna before she squared her delicate shoulders and allowed her gray eyes to meet her governess's clear pale blue orbs.

''Well, why then did you run away from your mama's house in the dead of night?'' Miss Corbett was moved to speak with a touch of impatience.

26

"Polly . . . she meant to marry me off to a man I have never met!" Shauna felt the wave of indignation take over again. "Now do you understand? I won't marry a stranger . . . I won't, and so I told her. She said that I must . . . that he was handsome and rich and would be good to me. Can you imagine? What do I care for riches or position? I have always thought that when I married it would be for love. . . ." Her shoulders drooped.

Polly took all this in with a growing frown. "She couldn't have meant it. Dearest, this start is most unlike Lady Elton. I can't believe she would force your hand . . . like this."

"Well, at first I did not think so, but she said all my chances of making a respectable match were ruined. She thought that all the mamas of marriageable prizes would not want me because of my long list of scandals. . . ."

"Why then did this . . . Who is he anyway?" Miss Corbett stuck in.

"Oh, I don't know, and I don't know why he didn't mind. Means to stick me in the country, no doubt, and who he is doesn't matter. Some titled London rake. Never mind that. We have to find something for me to do, for I shall never return to Mama's house. I . . . I can't trust her anymore. . . ."

"*You* can't trust *her*?" Miss Corbett was moved to astonishment. Her former charge's reasoning was intriguing. "You behave in a wayward fashion time and time again, and now you say you don't trust Lady Elton? Explain that to me if you can."

"Polly, don't you see? If I were to go back . . . things would be worse than ever. I have done yet another unforgivable thing. I have run away from home . . . in the middle of the night. By now all the servants know it. . . . And faith, if they know it, all of London will know it. I can never go back."

"Nonsense. Your servants have been led by you for as

long as I can remember. They are your people even more than they are Lady Elton's. They have always protected you even when you did not deserve it. Lady Elton, as distressed as she may be right now, has handled the situation so that no one need know that you are not at home.''

''I can't risk that. I can't go back. I am going to be a governess, and if you won't help me . . . I shall find someone who will. Mark me, Polly Corbett. I am determined in this.''

Miss Corbett knew that look. Shauna could be stubborn at times, and she could see that Shauna was in such a state. Perhaps what it needed was time. Perhaps Shauna was a touch spoiled and needed to know what life on the other side was like. This would take some thinking. She changed the topic for the moment and said casually, ''Of course, there is an explanation for that nice young man accompanying you to my home?''

In spite of herself, Shauna felt her cheeks go hot, and her color was not lost on Miss Corbett. ''Yes, well . . . that was very odd to be sure, and I can see how you might wonder, but . . . but there is a perfectly good explanation for it.''

''Yes, so there always is where you are concerned. I should be most interested to hear it.'' Miss Corbett eyed her with a twinkle.

Shauna did not meet Miss Corbett's eyes but found something on her quilt to occupy her interest as she answered, ''Oh well, he discovered me riding along in London and rather thought that I should not be allowed to head out for the New Forest alone.''

''Yes, so he said,'' returned Miss Corbett. ''I did, however, find him to be a gentleman and therefore am willing to allow the matter to drop for the time being . . . in spite of the fact that you were most improperly clothed and he was most certainly totally foxed!''

''Yes, he was terribly disguised . . . but better by the

time we reached your door. It must have been boys' night out or something." Shauna giggled.

Miss Corbett got to her feet, adjusted her mobcap round her short gray curls, and said, "When you have washed and dressed . . . and, Shauna, you may be in the country, but you are not to don britches"—she eyed Shauna warningly—"come to the garden, for I need to do some thinking."

Chapter Five

Lord Damien Drummond was announced, and Lady Elton put a wavering hand to her forehead. She followed this unconscious move with eyes heavenward before smiling in the direction of the door. She watched him as he strode forward and thought he looked rather haggard. Ah, but even so, he was certainly a very fine man. Just the sort Shauna would find attractive. Miserable creature—if only she had stayed to have herself a look.

She waited for Lord Drummond to bend over her hand and properly greet her before she attempted her carefully prepared speech. "My lord, I don't know how to break this to you—"

He interrupted with a frown and a soft "What is amiss?"

"Oh, naught, naught . . . well, actually . . . dearest Shauna is abovestairs with some dreadful childish malady. The doctor says it is not serious, but time-consuming . . . ."

"Time-consuming? I don't understand," he said, still frowning.

"Well, it is . . . the . . ." She fluttered with her expression and her hands. "I blush to say it . . ."

"Blush, then, and say it." His lordship was impatient.

She eyed him a moment and said, this time not looking

at him, "The measles, my lord. She is in no danger, but . . . of course cannot be seen for the time being . . ."

He found his eyebrow moving upwards. Fine, he thought, he was in no condition to be romantic at the moment anyway. He inclined his head and said with all the correct amount of sympathy in his voice, "I *am* sorry to hear this. . . . You will please send her my regrets."

"Yes, of course," breathed Lady Elton, thinking she had managed this matter very well.

"I shan't keep you." He was already bending over her hand again. "I am certain Miss Elton needs you."

"Thank you. You are most understanding, my lord." She watched him stride out of the room and felt herself relax a moment. Now, for mercy's sake, now what?

"So you see, Polly . . . do take me seriously," Shauna was pleading.

"I do see and I am taking you seriously," returned Miss Corbett gravely. "You are most welcome to stay on with me for as long as you like, but not until . . . I have returned."

Shauna stopped and eyed Miss Corbett. "Returned? Returned from where?"

Miss Corbett actually blushed and did not meet Shauna's straightforward gaze, but she did answer, "From my honeymoon."

"Honeymoon?" It was a shriek. It was followed by a clap of hands, and Shauna was throwing her arms around her Polly's plump body. "You are getting married! This is superb! This is wonderful!"

Polly smiled indulgently and said in a quiet voice, her eyes suddenly quite soft, "I think you will like Harry . . . very much."

"I am certain I shall, but what is important, Polly . . . is that you . . . like . . . love him?" Shauna eyed Miss

31

Corbett with some amusement, for there was something of the little girl in Miss Corbett's face.

"You are asking if, at my age, a woman can still fall in love, and the answer, my dearest heart, is yes. Perhaps not as wildly, or as blindly, as one can when one is in her first bloom . . . but most definitely, just as deeply."

Shauna dropped a kiss upon Miss Corbett's cheek and sighed, "I am so pleased . . . so very pleased."

Miss Corbett patted Shauna's hand and bade her sit down on the garden white-painted wrought-iron chair. "Yes, so am I, but it still leaves us in somewhat of a bind. Timing, as I said earlier—"

"Never mind that," broke in Shauna impatiently. "You haven't understood me yet."

"Haven't I?" Miss Corbett's brow was up.

"Dear Polly, I didn't mean to be rude, so don't get all ruffled. What I am trying to tell you is that I wish to hide away from Mama . . . from London . . . from Almack's . . . from all of them. I want to be a governess, and you can help me!"

Polly was startled. "Help you become a governess? Why, child, you have quite lost your darling mind!"

"No, I haven't . . . Polly . . . why couldn't I be a governess?" Shauna was pouting.

'For one thing, you are too young," returned Polly scathingly.

"No, I am not. I am one and twenty! You were twenty when you first started out. You told me that yourself!"

"Yes, but that was different. . . ." She waved off Shauna's interruption. "For another thing, you are far too beautiful. There is not a woman alive who would want you underfoot!"

"Nonsense . . . What have my looks to do with anything?"

"Everything. What woman would want a younger, lovelier creature tripping about her home and fascinating her husband? No, Shauna . . ." Polly was shaking her head. "It wouldn't work."

"Yes, but, Polly . . . I have all the skills . . . and I am good with children. Don't you remember how nicely I managed the Parson children . . . and the work I did at the orphanage near Elton?"

"Quite different. That was work suitable to your position. How could you go as a governess . . . under a false name? It wouldn't be right, Shauna. . . ." She turned her head as the sound of wheels ground over pebbles in the drive, and they looked across the white picket fence to find a handsome coach drawing up. "Why, who can that be?" said Polly softly as she surveyed the conveyance.

Shauna and Miss Corbett stood back and quietly watched as the coach came to a full stop. The door opened and an elderly gentleman clothed in sombre gray descended the steps, cane clasped in his gloved hand.

"Why, it is Mr. Trekner!" breathed Polly, and then with a wave of her hand, "Here, sir . . . in the garden!" To Shauna she commented, "I wonder what brings him here?"

The elderly man looked round at the sound of her voice and smiled warmly as he moved towards the white gate. "Miss Corbett!" he said as he tipped his hat and made his way to them. He bowed and said softly, "My, my . . . you are looking fit, Miss Corbett. How long has it been since I have seen you? Five . . . maybe six years?"

Polly laughed. "More like two, sir, and how nice to see you again, but what brings you to the New Forest?"

"You, indeed, you bring me," he answered her gravely.

"Really?" Her brows moved upwards and then she indicated the stone bench at her side, saying simultaneously, "Oh, how remiss of me. . . . Shauna, dear, here is an old friend of mine, Mr. Trekner."

The elderly man had removed his top hat as he sank onto the stone bench across from where Shauna was seated. He eyed her keenly for a moment as she smiled at him, but asked no questions. He had problems of his own to deal with. Miss Corbett offered refreshments, but he quickly declined, waving this off with his cane before setting it down. "There, there, Polly, don't fuss."

Polly eyed him doubtfully. Theirs was an old acquaintance. He had known her father, and he had been instrumental in Polly obtaining her first post as governess. She was not one to put things off, and inquired abruptly, "Well then, Mr. Trekner, what brings you here?"

He smiled appreciatively at her. "Ah, Polly, I need your help."

"Yes, of course, anything I can do . . ." she offered at once.

He looked at her boldly then. "Polly, I need you to do what you do best: manage a pair of wayward, unhappy children."

"My word, what can you mean?" she was surprised into asking.

"You will recall that I wrote to you and inquired whether your services as governess would be available for the Bromley twins?"

"Yes, yes . . ." she interrupted quickly, "and as I explained in my letter, I *am* retired. There were two very qualified ladies of my acquaintance that I did, however, recommend to you. . . ."

"So you did! Excellent girls, both of them! The twins ousted the first in less than six weeks. The second took them only one month to be rid of. The remuneration both were offered to reconsider and stay was quite exceptional, you know."

"Faith! Poor dears . . ." clucked Polly.

"Indeed, those two women were quite wretched when they left."

"No," she cut in, "I meant the children."

"The children?" He was certainly surprised.

"Yes, of course. Only think how very miserable and confused they must be."

"Then you will do it?" He was hopeful all at once.

She shook her head, "I am afraid that I cannot."

Despair could be seen in his aged eyes. "I am at my wits' end," he said quietly.

"Sir, dear sir, I would do it if it were at all possible. But I am about to be married this Sunday. . . ."

He looked at her with that and smiled. "Are you indeed? I *am* happy for you, Polly. Is he deserving?"

"I think so. . . ." she said softly.

Shauna worked up her courage and stuck in, "I will do it!"

Mr. Trekner and Polly both looked at her. He shook his head. "You are scarcely more than a child yourself."

"No, I am not a child, sir. I am one and twenty. Polly was twenty when she took on her first charge and I can do it! I know what it is to be a troubled child. . . . I could deal with them, and I am young and strong enough to handle what they can throw at me."

Again he shook his head. Shauna frowned and inquired, "Is it that you think their mother will not approve?"

"No, no. They lost their mother more than a year ago. That is the problem. They haven't any parental supervision, which is why I think you are just too young to handle the situation."

"I was raised to manage a household. I am skilled in French and Spanish. My math is poor, but my knowledge of literature is certainly enough for young children. . . . How old are they?"

"There are twins. A boy, Felix, and a girl, Francine. They are eight years old and full of mischief."

"Oh, please, sir, I can do it. I know I can. . . ." Shauna was pleading.

He was considering it. He was desperate. Polly was quiet during this duration. It occurred to her that this was perhaps just what Shauna needed to settle her own way-ward soul, and something instinctive told her Shauna was what the twins needed.

"Perhaps . . ." said Mr. Trekner, "but there are more."

"More what? Children?" Shauna was a bit surprised.

"In a manner of speaking, though they shan't trouble you. There is Mary. She is fourteen and presently up at finishing school, and there is Frederick. He is seventeen years old and presently attending Eton."

"If they haven't any parents . . . who is there with them now?" Shauna asked in some surprise.

"That is the problem. They are under the care of ser-vants. They have a half-brother from their mother's first marriage. He is Lord Drummond and is rarely at Bromley Grange," answered Mr. Trekner, again with a sigh. He looked at Polly for aid. "Well, what do you think?"

"Quite frankly, Mr. Trekner, I think that Shauna just might be the answer to your problem." She turned to Shauna and said sternly, "You are taking on a responsi-bility. You can't play with children's lives. Once started, girl, you must see it through."

"Polly, you know me. When I take something on, I always see it to its completion. I shan't leave these chil-dren stranded. When I leave them, they will be ready for me to go."

"What is all this talk of leaving?" Mr. Trekner eyed her from beneath heavy brows. "I haven't even said that you can have the position. . . ."

Shauna smiled at him. "Haven't you, sir?"

Polly released a sound something between a snort and a laugh. "Looks like we haven't any choice, Mr. Trekner. The children need someone to look after them, and I rather think Shauna just might fill that need."

Mr. Trekner cast his eyes towards the sky and silently prayed for peace.

Chapter Six

Two fair-haired children looked into one another's blue eyes and grimaced. "Well . . ." said the boy on a defiant note, "she won't stay. None of them do, and this one won't be any different."

His sister eyed him sadly. "I don't know, Felix. Maybe this one will like us. . . . Maybe it will be different. It might be nice to have someone—"

He pulled a face at her. "What's that you say? Someone to tell us what to do, when to go out . . . to keep us from the stables. . . ?" They were on their way at the moment to the stables, for horses were a passion with both of them.

"Hmmm. I shouldn't like to be kept from the horses, and that last governess was dreadful about it. . . ." mused his sister thoughtfully. "Still and all . . . this one is supposed to be a friend of Mr. Trekner's . . . and we do like *him*. . . ."

"What is that to say to anything?" he scoffed. "He is a man." As if this statement settled the matter, he proceeded, expecting the subject to be closed. It wasn't. His sister found herself needing, more and more, a woman to look after her, and cook just wasn't enough.

"Yes, but, Felix . . . if this one does turn out to be, er, pleasant, promise you won't put a frog in her bed like you did to the last."

He stopped in his tracks and exclaimed in some surprise, "But, Francie . . . that was funny. *You* laughed, too!"

"So I did, but she deserved a frog in her bed," returned his sister on a thoughtful note.

"And this one will get the same if she sends us off to bed without dinner!" retorted her brother, ready for battle.

She could see she was not getting anywhere and so decided to let the matter drop for the time being. At any rate, they had reached the large, rambling barn, and her frown vanished as she spotted their pony, Spike. Felix called his name out loud and squealed with delight as the pony raised his small head and returned their greeting with a snort. Thomas, the head groom, smiled and moved towards them.

"Seen Brown Glaze yet, darlin's?" Tom asked with a nod at them.

"Ay, that we did, Tom, but we didn't see any signs, " answered Felix with keen interest.

"Didn't ye now? Well, well . . . she be waxing, alright. Could be tonight."

"Tonight?" Francine shrieked. "Oh, Tom . . . we want to be there when she foals . . . please, please. . . ."

"Now, now . . . can't be spending the entire night in the barn, ye know. . . ."

"Yes, yes, we can . . . please, Tom." Felix joined Francine's pleading.

Something caught Tom's attention and he didn't answer them, but turned away instead. Felix frowned and called after him.

"Hush, lad!" commanded Thomas, on no ceremony with the child he had taught to ride even though he was but a servant.

"What? What is it?" Francine whispered.

Tom started off towards the stud paddock, calling their

prize stallion's name as he moved in that direction. "Frenchy! Eh, son, settle down."

Bromley Grange was certainly an impressive estate. Its lands were extensive and its parks neatly groomed, but it was not the extent of its landscape that caught Shauna's full interest. She pressed her piquant face to the coach window and exclaimed as she surveyed paddock after paddock of horses.

"Mr. Trekner! You never mentioned that Bromley Grange raised horses. Why . . . look at those mares. . . . They are quite beautiful. . . ."

"Hmmm. The estate brings in a handsome income from the animals."

"Stud paddocks must be in the back. . . ?" It was more a statement than a question.

"That's right. Like horses, do you? He was smiling at her. She was a lively bundle, and he had enjoyed his morning's ride with her.

"Like them? They are a passion. How many studs do they have?"

"French Connection is one," he said with a grin, and then laughed to see her mouth drop.

"Never say so! Why, he took more races last year than—"

"Quite so. Bold and Fancy is another."

"Why, this is beyond everything famous!" Shauna was moved to ejaculate, "Oh, look . . . their stables are superb! May we stop for just a moment before we go up to the house?"

He was anxious to find the twins and introduce them to Shauna. He was hopeful that she might prove to be just the sort of governess for the Bromley children, but he couldn't see that a short delay would do any harm. He sighed indulgently and agreed, taking up his cane and pounding at his driver's flooring, calling the man to halt the coach.

Shauna alighted and, though she wanted to fly into the barn, politely waited to take up Mr. Trekner's bent arm, and meekly walked beside him. However, she was not at his side for long. She heard the sound of a large horse in distress and, with a frown, broke away from Mr. Trekner and hurried down the corridor to the rear of the stable.

There, in one of the stud paddocks, she saw a magnificent stallion with all the room he needed at his back, and yet he had managed to cast himself in a corner between gate and flat rail! The stallion was groaning and thrashing, cutting his legs against the rail; there was a groom attempting to knock down one of the rails with a hammer, and there were two young children calling the stallion's name and attempting to calm him. The groom couldn't get too near the rail because of the flying hooves, and without a word Shauna ran back into the barn. Where were the other stableboys? None to be seen, but she managed to find the tack room and there grabbed two lunge lines. During this time, Mr. Trekner stood to one side and out of the way. Shauna took the lunge lines to the groom and, very much in command, said, "Here, take this. . . . Sling it round his front leg. I'll get his rear, and we'll get him over!"

"Aye . . . good girl!" said the groom. "But we still may need to get this rail out of the way."

"Right, but first we might be able to move him a bit. . . ."

They worked as a team and managed, without getting kicked, to get the lines around first the front leg and then the rear. Shauna looked toward the two children and called them to her. "Come on, loves . . . get behind me and pull me as I pull. . . ."

And so they pulled and in fact did manage to get him nearly over, but not quite. However, they had moved him

40

enough so that Thomas was able to now get close enough to remove the top flat rail. This done, they returned to pulling at the stud, who was now very nearly on his back. With a groan, Frenchy was over. He knew it and scrambled to stand, and blew for a moment.

Thomas shook his head and eyed Shauna. "Thankee, miss. . . . That was well done!"

She smiled. "However did such a brute find such a place?"

Thomas grinned. "See that mud in the corner? Frenchy, he likes to roll in mud, and I suppose there was no other about! Freak thing to happen. Oi'll be looking at his legs now. Good thing ye were 'ere. . . . All me lads are out and about this morning."

Shauna turned to the two children and touched their shoulders. "Well, and thank you! I didn't have the weight to manage that without your help."

They both blushed with pleasure, but this was short-lived, for Mr. Trekner broke the spell of the moment with reality. "Well, well, Felix. Francine! Come, we will all ride up to the house together. How nice that you are here to welcome your new governess!"

Shauna felt her heart sink when she witnessed their smiles vanish. She could have kicked Mr. Trekner in that moment, for she had had a feeling that these two were her future charges, and she could have wished that an introduction had come only after she had been able to converse with them. Ah well, she thought grimly, onward!

Chapter Seven

"Right," said Shauna with determination as she came back into the library and looked at the twins. She had just seen Mr. Trekner off, and here was the moment. She was going to have to win these two over, and she rather thought she knew the way. "I have a fancy to learn about Bromley. What say you if we take to horse and you take me under your wing and teach me about your beautiful home?"

The twins eyed one another in some stupefaction. Here was something new. This governess was asking them to teach her?

"Eh?" returned Felix doubtfully.

"Oh, can't you ride!" It was a taunt, though gently said.

"Of course we can ride!" Felix's chin was well up.

"Then . . . wouldn't you like to?" Shauna was all female.

"Well, yes . . . I mean . . ." Felix stumbled over his thoughts. His sister intervened with practicality.

"But . . . do you have a riding habit? None of our other governesses did." Francine was eyeing Shauna gravely.

"Ah, there is the rub," said Shauna cheerfully. "Do you think you will be ashamed of me if I hop up as I am?" She was wearing her simple light blue traveling gown, but she had on her half boots, which she had worn

42

the night she rode out on her Bessy. "I suppose I shall have to ride a lady's saddle, though I would rather ride astride."

"Ride astride?" Felix was astounded. "Girls can't ride astride!"

"Oh, but they can, and I do very often; however, I suppose the proprieties must be observed now that I am a governess, and I shall ride a lady's saddle." She smiled at both of them.

"Is . . . is this the first time you were ever a governess?" Francine asked in some awe.

"It is," answered Shauna promptly. "So you must help me, you see, and tell me when I do something very wrong, for I understand you two have experience with these things."

Felix and Francine eyed one another again. This was turning out to be a nightmare, thought Felix, for he almost liked this strange creature!

"Well, is it agreed, then? Shall we ride?" asked Shauna brightly.

"Oh yes," breathed Francine, already enchanted.

Felix was made of sterner stuff. He put on a frown and said, "Come on then, let's not take all day over the thing!" with which he led the way.

"Right," said Shauna, taking up Francine's ready hand and following.

Freddy Bromley was seventeen. He was fair, he was tall, lean, and up to every rig. He was mischievous and full with his need for adventure. He was also the firstborn Bromley male and therefore held the title. His young lordship had over the past year acquired a sense of self and felt that he had no one but himself to answer to . . . and perhaps his older half brother, Damien. He worshipped Damien, but then Damien was scarcely about, and thus he pushed this concern aside when he found himself in disgrace at Eton.

Shrugging his shoulders, he made his leisurely way home, stopping along the way to dally with various sporting individuals he had met during his journey. He could not see that he had done anything so very dreadfully wrong, at least nothing that should have caused such a fuss. At any rate, he was confident that Damien would not be at Bromley and perhaps would never find out about his lapse in conduct and education. Such is youth.

He found Tom at the stables and gave the elderly groom a hearty greeting as he handed over his horse, saying that the gelding should be properly pampered, having been on the road for the last three days. Off he went to the house, shouting for the twins once inside. There he was affectionately greeted by Thurston, the butler, and advised that the twins had gone off riding with their new governess.

"Gone off riding, you say?" Freddy was surprised. "With their new governess?"

"Yes, m'lord."

"But . . . does she ride?" Freddy's eyes were open wide and his fair brows were high. "We have nothing in our stables that is suitable for . . . a prim old governess, you know."

"Well, as to that . . . Miss Corbett didn't seem . . . well, she is not quite like any of the other governesses the children have had in the past, m'lord."

"No? Well . . . perhaps I'll just go and have a look for m'self," announced his young lordship, with some interest and curiosity in his blue eyes.

Prancer was a dark bay with a white blaze and two white stockings. He was a fine-looking piece of horseflesh, and he was true to his name. Shauna had left her own dear Bessy with Polly, as a governess could not very well bring in her own livestock, but she took one look at Prancer and fell in love. She cooed to him, and Felix said pugnaciously, "Don't think to ride him. Mary never could, and Freddy says he is too raw for him to bother with."

"Yes, but Mary doesn't like any horse with spirit. . . ." put in Francine, who liked Prancer as well but had not yet been given permission to ride anything other than her pony.

"Tom . . ." said Shauna with a smile at the groom, "if you will have Prancer saddled for me, I think I shall try and give him some exercise."

Tom looked her over and remembered her skill with the cast stallion. He smiled and said that he would have one of the livery boys see to it at once. It wasn't long afterwards that Shauna and the children were mounted and making their way to the bridle path through the woods adjacent to Bromley Park.

Prancer danced about at first and worked himself into a lather. Shauna sat him well, patted his neck, and cooed to him softly. His ears moved to the sound of her voice as she walked him along. The children watched her handle the spirited gelding, and even Felix found himself admiring her skill. She asked the children questions about their home, the breeding, the racing that Bromley was famous for, and discovered they were two very adorable beings, lonely and in need of caring. Her heart went out to them.

As they returned to the stables, Shauna smiled at Felix and said, "What do you think of Prancer now?"

"Hmmm," admitted the young man with a frown, "he seems to like you . . . but Freddy says he needs refinement."

"Freddy knows what he is talking about," said Shauna sagaciously, for she guessed that Freddy was someone dear. "Who is Freddy?"

"Freddy?" Felix indicated by his expression some concern for Shauna's intelligence. "He is Lord Bromley, my brother!" He shook his head. "Don't you know anything about us?"

"Felix!" reproved his sister. "That is rude. How is Miss Shauna to know anything about us when she has only just arrived?"

"Well . . ." shrugged her twin, "that Miss Adler knew all about us, and so did—"

"Never mind them," cut in his sister. She turned to Shauna with eyes ready to adore and said, "We have a sister, too—Mary. She is nearly fifteen and she is up at school. Mary is pretty, but she is nothing to you. . . ."

Her brother made a disgusted sound but managed to eye Shauna from reluctant eyes, and said, "I will tell you what, though. You won't last!"

"Won't I?" returned Shauna, smiling indulgently at him. "Perhaps not. I have never liked to stay where I was not wanted. . . . It's a dreadful feeling."

Felix eyed her scathingly at this, but something inside him moved. He knew what it was not to be wanted. He had never thought anyone older felt that way. Adults all seemed to have a place in the world.

"We want you," returned Francine, and then to her brother, "Don't we, Felix?"

Felix glanced Shauna's way and said gruffly, "No matter what we want. When my other brother . . . Lord Drummond . . . has a look at you . . . out you'll go!"

Francine frowned over this and sighed, "Felix has a point there, Miss Shauna. Damien is bound to think you . . . too young to take care of us. He will say—" she cut herself off as something caught her eye in the distance. "Felix . . . look there, 'tis Freddy! Freddy!" She shouted her brother's name and stood in the stirrups to wave in the air before putting her pony into a gallop.

The sudden movement spooked Prancer so that he hopped a rear and attempted to take off as well. Shauna worked her reins, cursed her sidesaddle, and sat him well enough to catch hold of him. The effort took her breath

46

away and accentuated her youthful vitality so that Freddy's first vision of Shauna sent him reeling into infatuation.

"Freddy!" Francine was already off her pony and flinging herself into her brother's ready arms.

"Hallo, brat!" He gave her a squeeze and looked up to find Felix standing before him. "And you, little man!"

Felix seemed to take this as an invitation, and it was with great affection that he held out his hand in greeting. "Freddy, it's good to have you home." So saying, he dropped his attempts at maturity and dove at his brother.

Freddy smiled and then requested an introduction as Shauna dismounted and came forward.

"Freddy . . . this is Miss Shauna Corbett. She has only just arrived today to be our new governess. . . ." Francine frowned. "Does that mean she is yours, too . . . since you are home now?"

Freddy nearly choked, but he managed to restrain the answer that came to his lips. He shot his sister a scathing look and turned to Shauna. "How do you do? You handle him well; I was never really able to get Mary to ride him, and he doesn't seem to like men."

"He certainly is full of spirit, but I think all he needs is consistent work." She smiled at Freddy. "Tell me, my lord, how do you happen to be home from Eton so early in the season?"

"Zounds, you do come to the point!" he chuckled, and then met her gaze. "Sent home in disgrace."

"Were you?" responded Shauna. "How very exciting. What did you do, let a monkey loose in the dining hall?"

He laughed. "Egad! What a wonderful notion. No, far more common than that. I was caught climbing through my window . . . after hours."

She eyed him a moment. "Well, that is breaking the rules, but one doesn't usually get sent home—"

He cut her off. "For the third time and after a very severe warning."

47

"Freddy . . ." Clearly Felix was disgusted. "How could you let yourself get caught . . . three times?"

"Ay," sighed Freddy, "but when one considers that it was three out of perhaps ten . . . twelve nightly excursions in one month, one doesn't feel so badly." He was smiling broadly.

Felix touched his older brother's arm and pronounced him to be "a complete hand."

"Now, just a moment . . ." put in Shauna, surprised at herself, for such pranks were right up her alley and had always been her style, "getting oneself expelled is not what a Bromley owes himself or his name. . . ." Her tone was severe, and she eyed first Freddy a warning and then Felix.

Felix looked at the ground; Freddy looked at Shauna and made up his mind that anything she said was perfectly right with him. "Point taken, Miss Shauna. . . . but I can't regret it, for if I hadn't gotten caught and been sent down, I wouldn't be here now . . . with you. . . ."

"Aw, Freddy . . ." complained Felix, watching his brother turn into a Don Juan.

"I am famished," announced Francine. "It must be time for tea. . . ."

Chapter Eight

Lord Drummond sat back against his high-backed leather-upholstered desk chair and surveyed the stout, prune-faced man standing before him. Trouble here, he thought as he smiled and indicated the chair at his side.

"Do be seated, Dr. Hendricks, and tell me what brings you here." It was cordially said, but there was that touch of reserve, that warning in his voice that kept people just a bit wary. Dr. Hendricks was subject to the man and tempered his words as he took up the chair.

"Your brother . . . your half brother, my lord, brings me here," he said portentously.

"Indeed, how so?" Damien's mobile brow was up and his blue eyes were sharp.

"His behavior, my lord, is next to unpardonable, and what makes it worse is his cavalier attitude. He doesn't seem to care that he was sent down . . . makes no—"

"Sent down?" Damien cut in with sudden acuteness. He had unconsciously sat forward.

"Ah, so it matters then? I was beginning to wonder."

"Matter? Of course it matters! What the devil are you talking about, man?" His lordship had lost patience.

Dr. Hendricks shrank back a touch, concerned that he had overstepped. The truth was that he liked Freddy Bromley and thought if only some attention was directed toward the boy from his lordship, he might yet apply himself. At the same time, he was a realistic man and did not want to make an enemy of Drummond. "It is just that I have written to you on two occasions and did not receive a reply. . . ."

"Wrote to me? I never received any letters." Damien frowned over this. "To where were the letters addressed?"

"I had them franked to Bromley Grange, and the thing is . . . when I was there and inquired about them, it seems the Bromley servants held them there for you, thinking perhaps you were due to stop in and see your young twins." There was a trace of censure in his tone.

Damien was beyond the age where he flushed; however, he did so now. The twins. He had not seen them in months. It was deplorable. He turned away and paced a step. "I am not often at Bromley" was his quiet answer.

"So I was given to understand. The thing is . . . Freddy should have been there by now, but when I arrived there yesterday afternoon, he had not yet been received. What is more, those twins of yours seem to run wild about the place. When I inquired about them, I was told that your man went off to fetch their new governess." He was eyeing Damien thoughtfully, taking his measure, for he could see that his lordship was distressed by all this news. It didn't quite make sense. If Lord Drummond cared, why had he allowed things to come to such a pass?

"The twins are soon going to be under my direct supervision," his lordship responded curtly. "And as to Freddy . . . he, too, will soon find that he must alter his style!" He continued to pace, brought himself up short, and eyed Hendricks. "Tell me, sir, if you will, was Freddy's offense such that he will not be allowed to return to school?"

Dr. Hendricks shook his head. "Thank the saints, that is not so; however, such a possibility could occur in the future if he does not settle down and apply himself to his studies instead of the frivolous larks he seems to embark upon every other day.''

"Thank you.'' Lord Drummond was moving round to his desk, taking up a quill, jotting down something quickly. "Do stay and enjoy some refreshments, Dr. Hendricks. I shall have them sent in to you, but I know you will forgive me for not staying to bear you company. It seems I have been remiss in my own behavior, and Freddy's cavalier attitude stems from my own.'' He had now moved to the study door and opened it wide. "I mean to handle the situation . . . immediately!''

"You leave for Bromley?'' Dr. Hendricks inquired after him, only slightly surprised.

"Yes, sir, that I do.''

"My lord. . . .?'' Hendricks called him to a halt. "A moment, please?'' He waited for his lordship to pause and turn his attention to him before he smiled apologetically. "I would appreciate it greatly if you would send me word. I shall be returning to Eton tomorrow morning, and I would like to know that Freddy is at least home and under your . . . er . . . direction.''

"Done! And, Hendricks . . . thank you.'' So saying, his lordship was already calling for his livery.

"Here, let me help you with that. . . .'' said Freddy, jumping to assist Shauna in moving the children's writing table across the room.

She allowed him and stepped back to view this handiwork thoughtfully. "That's better,'' she pronounced with some satisfaction, and then to the twins, "Don't you think?''

Felix eyed the desk, the sun streaming in from the window, and then the open books that reposed on the desk, and shrugged his shoulders. "I suppose,'' he conceded.

"Why, 'tis much better,'' stuck in Francine happily.

"The table should always have been there in the light. Some days it is so dreary in here. . . ." She looked round and sighed, "May we not go down to the pond to see the ducklings . . . before the day is lost . . . please, Miss Shauna?"

She smiled at them. It was already too late into the day to expect them to do anything further on their books, and the outing would do them all some good. "Indeed . . . I think so."

Felix eyed her suspiciously. This female was too good to be true, and he was apt to be suspicious. "Now then?"

"Now," she laughed. "But first fetch your spencer, Francie; I'll just get my shawl."

"The pond is beautiful at this time of year. I can't wait to show it to you," put in Freddy dreamily.

"Yes, of course, the pond!" returned Shauna, forming a notion. "There is a great deal that can be learned at a pond. We can manage two birds with one stone, as the saying goes. . . ." She laughed at Freddy's expression and waved him off. "Go on . . . you go and fetch the biscuits for the ducks."

"At once!" he answered dramatically, and was off, happy to be of service, for he was already quite infatuated with the new governess.

The walk to the pond was done with everyone conversing in French. Shauna made a game of it, starting it with a song and then presenting the simplest of questions, requiring only a basic answer in the French tongue, so that even Felix became quite enthralled. By the time they had reached the pond, she had started a short story, embellishing it with romance, keeping it simple enough for them to understand, sticking in a word of English here and there to help them along, and ending it with the promise to continue it the next day when they had learned additional French vocabulary.

They stopped to view the pond and Shauna exclaimed,

"Why, it is everything you said, Freddy. Quite, quite beautiful!"

"Look!" shrieked Felix, and took after something in a great rush.

"Oh no . . ." wailed Francine, ". . . he will catch it and shake it in my face."

"What? What will he shake in your face?" Shauna was wide-eyed, for she could see that Felix had indeed caught something, and was stroking it and bringing it towards them.

"It's a frog!" announced Felix proudly, and though he did not wriggle it before his cringing sister, he did put it toward Miss Shauna with great glee.

"No," said Miss Shauna calmly, and proceeded to amaze her young charge by putting an ungloved finger out to stroke the amphibian's head, "not just a frog, Felix, but a bullfrog!"

Freddy burst into indecent mirth, and Felix's mouth dropped open. "A . . . bullfrog. . . ?" He eyed her suspiciously. "How do you know?"

"Why . . . look at his size. He will live for about fifteen years, you know." She smiled to see him look at her oddly before he set the creature down and stood back to watch him hop off and away.

Miss Shauna was fast breaking down all of Felix's defenses, and at the moment he was at a loss. Just how does one react to such a governess? She actually touched a frog!

Chapter Nine

Lord Damien Drummond strode through the front door and handed the butler his driving coat, gloves, and hat, smiled amicably at the man, and inquired sharply, "Tell me, Thurston, has my brother Frederick been heard from?"

"Why yes, my lord. He arrived yesterday."

"Did he, by God! Well, that is something. Where is he presently?"

"He is with the children and the new governess, my lord."

"New governess? Will wonders never cease! So that is another accomplishment. What sort of woman is she, Thurston? Do the children like her?"

"I must say, my lord, she is unlike any governess we have had here before. As to the children liking her, well, she has only been here since yesterday, but yes, I rather think even Felix seems taken with her."

"Really? Where are they now?" His lordship was intrigued.

"At the pond, my lord, er . . . feeding the ducks. . . ."

The door swung open wide and Freddy stepped aside to allow Miss Shauna, her shawl full with a crew of wriggling yellow fluffs, to pass before him. Behind her, Francine was squealing with delight and interjecting, "Be

54

careful. . . . Oh, Miss Shauna . . . one is escaping. . . .''
with which she grabbed at the shawl and held it together
where one little duckling had managed to stick out its head.

However, Shauna was struck into such immobility that
all she could do was stare at the tall and arresting man
before her. What was *he* doing here? Faith, but he was the
most handsome man she had ever seen, and how very
exciting to see him again! The night he had ushered her
into his carriage and taken her to Polly Corbett's came
flooding into her mind's eye and brought the blush to her
cheek. How he had kissed her! How she had let him kiss
her. Now here she was, no longer a member of the haute
ton, but a governess. . . . And what would he think?

His lordship was thunderstruck. That night was more of
a cloud of illusions in his mind, for he had been badly
dipped, but he did remember her, and vividly. Here she
was, and oddly enough, he felt a sudden rush of desire.
Ridiculous! And what the deuce was she doing with his
twin charges? She was far too young to be a governess
. . . far too pretty. This was absurd. This was intolerable.

''Damnation!'' he was moved to utter.

This induced a giggle from Shauna, who found her voice
with her sense of humor, and answered him by asking,
''Pardon, sir, what was that you said?''

''Never mind!'' he growled. It was all he was able to
return, for the twins had screamed his name with delight
bordering on wildness and had by then encased him in
their arms. He found himself touched, and he looked down
on their pale gold heads of hair and said, ''Come then,
monkeys. We have some catching up to do.''

Over them he gazed sternly at Frederick and said, ''You
and I will talk presently, so I trust you will await me in
the library.'' He didn't need a reply, for his tone was such
that none would oppose him. To do so would be folly, and
so Frederick knew. He gulped, and though he was white
and felt his knees weaken, he managed to nod and say

with a show of cavalier bravado, "And greetings to you, too, my brother, Damien."

His lordship's eyebrow flew up, but he restrained the heady retort that sprang to his lips. He was not equipped to deal with youths. He had never been in such a position. He did not feel quite old enough at eight and twenty to chastise a younger brother for behavior that had been so similar to his own. Instead, he turned then to Shauna and said in stern accents, "Ours is an interview that should have taken place before you were installed here at Bromley. However, even though it will have to be delayed still further for the moment, it is a meeting that will take place."

Shauna wanted to giggle. His gravity was at such variance with the Damien who had entertained her the night he had delivered her to Polly. But though her gray eyes twinkled, she managed a solemn tone. "Indeed, I look forward to it, though you seem a touch sterner by the light of day. . . ." Her voice trailed off and did in fact take on the hint of a giggle as she moved towards the kitchen.

His eyes flashed and something inside of him sparkled to reply. He controlled himself. This was no behavior for a governess. He called after her, "Such levity of mind is *not* becoming in a governess."

"Is it not? How odd that you should think so. I have always found levity . . . in anyone . . . a becoming trait." So saying, she did indeed release a pent-up gurgle of laughter as she sped down the hall with the ducklings.

Freddy started to chuckle, encountered his brother's freezing glare, and fell into a deprecatory cough. His young sister sighed adoringly and said, "Damien . . . she is wonderful. Don't you think she is wonderful?"

"Eh?" returned Damien, who had just been thinking this was one more governess who would have to go. "No, no, little one, I do not!"

Francine's eyes flew open wide with shock and sudden fear. She stamped her foot at him. "Well, she is!"

He was surprised. "And you, Felix . . . Are you of the same mind?"

Felix was not about to describe any governess in such fabulous terms; however, he did drop his eyes to the ground, shuffle his feet, and grumble, "Well . . . she is a sight better than the others we've had."

"Is she, indeed?" returned Damien, frowning darkly. "Well, we shall watch her and see."

Chapter Ten

The interview his lordship had so ominously promised Shauna came some twenty minutes before the dinner hour at Bromley. She was just fussing in her small room over the only other dress she had brought into the country with her. It was a simple thing of dark blue silk and showed to advantage her provocative lines. Not at all suitable for a governess, though its scoop neckline was not as deeply cut as some of her other gowns at home. What to do? Brave it out. What else could she do? She braced herself and made her way belowstairs and to the library.

Thurston opened the library door for her as he had been instructed and gently announced her presence before he quietly withdrew and closed the door after him. Shauna folded her hands together and let them rest at her waist as she met his lordship's gaze. What eyes he had. Even in the dim light they glittered bright blue. How sensuous were his lips. . . .

"Well, and though you look . . . ravishing . . ." he said softly, "you do not look the part."

"Nevertheless, I think I can play it," she answered immediately.

"And is that what you are doing?" He had moved closer to her and was all too aware of the softness of her smile as she came into the room and steadily met his gaze.

"Isn't that something we all do?" She was enjoying herself, watching him, teasing him away from his shields.

"Don't play at semantics with me. I want answers," he returned sharply.

"Ah, then you must give me questions," she answered pertly, and brought herself close enough to look up at his face and allow his blue eyes to discover the light in her gray ones.

He was certainly attracted to this woman, he thought irritably, and frowned at her. "Right then, have a seat and I will put them to you."

She took up the lady's chair near the fire and folded her hands in her delicate lap, demurely waiting. He came to tower over her and decided instead to pull up a chair near her.

"Right then. I shall come to the point. When we met . . . you were fleeing London, for reasons of your own, and going to your relative. . . ." He hesitated and she immediately urged him on.

"Y-yes?"

"I suppose you did not then know you were to take on a position as governess?"

"No. I only knew I had to get to Polly. . . ." she answered softly.

"How then did you come to be at Bromley?"

"Your man . . . Mr. Trekner came to enlist my Polly to be governess to the twins. She could not oblige . . . . and I could," Shauna answered simply.

"How old did you say you were?"

"I am one and twenty," she answered easily, her eyes lighting up.

"You don't look it. Why . . . you look—" he started.

"Old enough to kiss," she stuck in quickly.

She had shocked him into silence for a moment, but this he waved aside with a testy "That is quite different!"

"Is it?" She tilted her pretty head. "Thank you, I shall

59

try to remember that. . . . But do you think you might explain in what way it is different?''

''Never mind!''

''Right, my age, then, is no longer in question,'' she returned promptly. ''What then is?''

''Your experience!'' he retorted superiorly, thinking he had her now.

''Ah, I must say, I have none. I have had an extensive education, however, and I do so like children, but if you feel that perhaps you need someone else, someone with experience, well then, I shall leave.'' She was calling him out and was surprised to find her heart so very afraid of what he might do.

Here now was the problem. He couldn't send her off. The twins did seem to like her, which was a feat no other governess since their mother's death had been able to accomplish. Yet how was he going to have her underfoot and not seduce the chit? He would have to keep away from her. Perhaps go back to London as soon as he could. Still, he had promised himself after visiting with the twins that he would stay on for some days at least, as they did seem to need him. Right, he would just keep his distance from this pretty little minx.

''No, I don't think you should leave. I think we shall give this a chance and hope for the best. The twins do seem to want you to stay on, and children do learn more from someone they can like and admire.''

She started to her feet. ''Thank you. If you will excuse me, I will go up to have dinner with them now.''

''No. I want them to have dinner with me while I am here, and you shall, of course, join us . . . family style.''

Gray eyes met blue and then Shauna's lashes lowered shyly. It occurred to her that she was here under a false name, under false pretexts, and how really dreadful that was. She would have to make it come out right, somehow.

* * *

Cook was a large woman, full of warmth and motherly tendencies. She had taken Shauna under her wing almost at once. It was not the norm for an under-servant to behave in such a fashion with a governess whose rank was one of the highest in the household. However, Shauna was no ordinary governess. Cook had mused over this fact as their first week with Miss Shauna passed.

Shauna took up a freshly baked cookie from the cookie sheet and started to nibble. Cook snatched it from her hands and chided her at once, "You will ruin your lunch!" She turned and found herself nearly stepping on one of the ducklings as it scurried across her floor. "And look here, these things have to go, Shauna my love! Do ye hear me, child? Enough is enough!"

"But, Bess . . . the twins do so love to nurse them, and . . . it is such a dangerous world out there for them without a mother to look after them. . . ." Shauna pleaded.

"Whist now . . . we are speaking of ducks . . . just ducks!"

At the open doorway his lordship came to an abrupt stop and listened to this interchange. Shauna had wreaked an undefinable change at Bromley. Everywhere her presence was felt. He had come in search of the twins, for he had promised to take them to the fair that was just outside of town. The kitchen, he was told, was where Miss Shauna had been seen going toward, and where Miss Shauna was, the twins were nearly always sure to be. She had been at Bromley a week; they had had her influence for only this short time, and already he could see such a change in them, even in Felix.

"Just ducks? Fie on thee, Bess!" laughed Shauna, snatching the cookie back from her waving hand. "They are babes . . . orphan babes. . . ."

"And they certainly do not belong underfoot!" put in his lordship as he entered the room and smiled at Shauna.

He bent to pick one up and stroke it. "Bess is right; they are certainly getting too large and too unmanageable for her in the kitchen. They will be safe enough in the stables."

Shauna was aware that once again his entrance had the strange effect of taking her breath away. She had to overcome this heady feeling whenever she was in his presence. She put down the cookie, for all at once she couldn't eat, and said, "If you think so, then it is done." She began scooping up the escaped ducklings and setting them back in the basket. There were four in all, and the last was still in his hands. She took up the basket and moved to him, waiting for him to deposit his handful.

His eyes nearly stunned her with the force of their rich blue color, with the grip of their vitality. She lowered her lashes, which allowed him a moment to note how dark they were against her lovely cheeks. She felt his gaze and raised her lashes so that he could see her gray eyes alight with dancing flecks of hot gold. Desire spun through him; she felt it, and it was like a bolt of lightning that ran through them both. He set the duckling down and regained control of himself.

"The twins?" he said, and his tone was formal. "Have you managed to get them ready?"

"Yes. They are only just outside playing hide-and-seek," she answered softly.

"They shouldn't be off playing when I asked you to have them ready to leave with me at noon!" he returned a touch too sharply. He heard his voice and nearly winced at his sternness.

"Yes, my lord." She smiled sweetly, though she wanted to grit her teeth. "But it is nearly half past noon, and they were getting restless. They aren't far."

"I see," he returned, and went to the garden doors to call them. They appeared a moment later, rosy-cheeked and out of breath, both of them smiling. "Ready, monkeys?" he laughed, for they looked adorable and happy.

"Yes, oh yes," answered Francine, going to touch Shauna's hand. "You had better fetch your spencer, though, Miss Shauna. There is a rough nip in the air." Francine had learned to adore Shauna and, oddly enough, had adopted quite a motherly attitude in her governess's regard.

Shauna blushed. "Oh no, love. This outing is for you and Felix." In her embarrassment she took an unconscious step backward.

His lordship was aware of her reticence and experienced a pang of guilt. He had spent the week making it clear to her that she was no more than a servant.

"You'll like it," said Felix in his matter-of-fact way. "No point being missish, for you are not, Miss Shauna. We want you there, and so does Damien. . . ." He looked at his brother, and there was just the hint of a challenge there. "Don't you, Damien?"

"You are most welcome to join us," said Damien coldly.

Contrariness prompted Shauna to accept. "Thank you, you are most kind, my lord."

"Is he?" stuck in Freddy, coming into the kitchen at that moment. "About what? And why the deuce is everyone in the kitchen? What is going on?"

"Going to the fair!" answered Francine, going to take Freddy's hand. "Will you come?"

"Oh, I don't know. . . ." Freddy answered slowly, for he saw an opportunity to be alone at Bromley with Shauna.

"There is a performing bear," announced Felix. "You will like that, Freddy."

"Yes, but I have seen performing bears. . . ." answered Freddy, staring worshipfully at Shauna.

"I will just be a moment, then, while I go and fetch my cloak," said Shauna, excusing herself.

"What? Are you going out?" asked Freddy, concerned.

"Why . . . to the fair." She smiled and moved towards the exit.

"To the fair. . . ? Ah, of course, the fair. Wonderful place. Think I will go have a look in at the performing bear after all!"

"Oh, Freddy . . ." laughed his young sister, ". . . you are looking more like a widgeon every day."

Chapter Eleven

The fair proved to be a wonderful place indeed. There were pies, swings, toys for sale, and all sorts of things to fascinate a child. There were tents that hawkers called bakers' booths, and fruit booths. There were tents that advertised entertainment for adult men. There was a fortune-teller, and there certainly was a performing bear.

This proved to be good fun for the entire company, including Damien, and they left this tent in good spirits.

"A candy apple . . . please, Damien. . . ?" begged Francine.

Her brother smiled, flipped her a coin, and told them affectionately not to get lost. Freddy was torn between staying at Shauna's side and making his way to a group of cronies to shoot the breeze for a few minutes. She settled the matter for him. "Freddy . . . that looks to me like a group of your friends. . . ?"

"Them. . . ? Never mind them," he answered gallantly.

"Silly . . . go to them before they make themselves hoarse calling you," she laughed.

Sheepishly, he excused himself, "Well . . . just for a moment then." To his older brother he charged, "You will take good care of our treasure, eh, Damien? I won't be long."

"Treasure indeed!" returned his lordship caustically, and turned to find wide gray eyes staring reproachfully at him.

"That is very rude, but I daresay 'tis true that quality gentry such as yourself don't think we poor lower classes have any feelings." She was having a jolly good time.

He felt color flood his cheeks and then he went white. "I beg your pardon. . . . I did not mean that as a slur against you. I was merely trying to bring him to order. His . . . interest in you is far too marked to be tolerable."

"For either of us, but I rather think his . . . interest, as you put it, is just that, and only for the moment. It will pass with time."

"That remark . . ." he stuck in on a frown, ". . . what you said about the quality not being aware that the lower classes have feelings . . ."

"Y-es?" She avoided his eyes, for hers were alight with laughter.

"I don't mean to dispute that with you, but I question your right to the platform. Are you not a member of the aristocracy? And . . . Shauna . . . please do not pitch any gammon at me. Your speech, your walk, your manners . . . your style all denote your higher station, yet—"

"Yet I am a governess. A mystery, my lord?"

"Indeed, a mystery. Will you clear it up?"

"No, I don't think so, my lord. You have been curt to me; that is, when you are not ignoring me. You have been rude to me and you have been coldly neglecting the fact that I have been able to help your brother and sister through a difficult time in their lives. I have learned to care for them, not because it is my duty, but because of the affection I feel for them both. I am just their governess, I know, but you treat me as though I don't exist. If I had been old, dowdy, and with less youth and more experience, you might have been kinder to me. You have not judged me on my merits, my lord, but on my looks. Tell me, what is a young woman with some countenance to do in this world? Must she always sell herself because men like you think she is too young and pretty to be a governess? That is unfair and cruel. Why should I confide anything about myself to you?"

He was taken aback. They had been walking slowly together, and he found they were standing near a narrow tent aisle. He took her arm and pulled her to one side. "Shauna . . . you are forgetting our first meeting, what influence that had over me!"

"I am not forgetting that. I am not forgetting your very delightful kisses that night, and I am not forgetting your willingness to deliver me to my . . . er . . . to Polly." Faith, she thought, she had almost said, to her governess. "You were, even in your"—she smiled—"fuzzy state of mind, most gallant, for you did manage to leave me . . . very nearly untouched. I trusted you . . . and you were a gentleman."

Damn, he thought, watching her flitting expressions, she was a beauty. She was pert, she was alluring, she was like a mesmerizing charm, drawing her closer. He wanted her. Desperately, he wanted her. Before he could think this out, before he could stop himself, he had her in his arms and his mouth closed on hers. When he let her go it was to flash at her in a rough tone, "Don't you understand, I haven't forgotten that night either, and perhaps I have regretted leaving you . . . untouched!"

Shauna knew what she wanted, and it wasn't this. For some days now, she had known her feelings for Damien Drummond. She wasn't going to allow him to kiss her in an alleyway. He thought her a servant, and she would have him treat her like a "gentry mort." She would have him fall in love with her while she was a governess at Bromley. She would have him propose marriage, not a discreet affair. Even though she was a governess, such was her romantic fantasy. She pulled out of his hold.

"Don't regret it; you spared me"—there was a tease in her bright gray eyes—"so that I might yet come to Bromley . . . whole and virginal"—she laughed to see the shocked response to her frankness—"and care for Felix and Francine." She lowered her lashes and moved forward and out of the alleyway. How difficult to move away from his touch. How very difficult. It took all her self-control.

He was fevered for this gray-eyed minx! He wanted her. There was something about her, more than her pretty face, her provocative body. There was just something about her every movement that arrested his attention. Fire and hell! He had never wanted a woman the way he wanted this black-haired vixen governess. This was insane!

"Right then, Freddy . . ." Shauna patted the empty spot on the stone seat. Wild roses were just beginning to bloom at her back, and the entire picture was fetching. He could not resist, even in his preoccupation, and he went to her, dropping down heavily and sighing without realizing that he was doing so. "What is it, dear? You have been . . . somber all afternoon. What happened at the fair . . . someone annoy you?"

"Why do you say that?" he asked sharply.

"Because I noticed your change of mood as soon as you returned from your friends . . . and then on the ride home. . . ." She peeped at him in her enchanting way. "That is why I lured you into the garden . . . to get you to confess all. . . ."

He gave her a wry smile and said gravely, "And that is what it would be . . . a confession. . . ." Then, bracing himself up, "Gentlemen don't burden ladies with their problems."

"Well, there is no doubt in my mind that you stand very much a gentleman, sir . . . but I"—her hand went to her

bosom as she inclined her head—"am more than a lady."
She smiled up at him.

He colored up and stammered, "Wh-what do you
mean. . . ?"

"I mean that I am your senior by several years. I am
your brother and sister's governess, and therefore hold
some position of authority and might be depended on to
help . . . all of you." She finished her sentence softly.

He reached out and touched her hand. "Thank you,
Miss Shauna, but . . . this is something I must work out
for myself."

She didn't want to press him just at that moment. Gently
she withdrew the hand he was squeezing and said, "Well
then, onward. It is nearly the moment of high tea, young
man, and I for one stand in need of it."

He laughed, stood up, and waited for her to rise and
move forward, stopping short when he came upon his older
brother, who had been standing stock still on the garden
path. "Damien!" he said in some surprise. "I didn't see
you there."

"Obviously," said his lordship dryly.

"We were just going in for tea. . . ." said Freddy on a
somewhat nervous note. He had his own reasons to be
anxious about his brother's hovering presence, and these
reasons had naught to do with his being observed in the
garden with Miss Shauna.

"Good. Go along then. . . . I will bring Miss Shauna
in with me, as I wish to have a few words with her re-
garding the twins." Clearly he had dismissed Freddy, and
there was naught for the young man to do but retreat,
which he did with more haste than the occasion called for.

"Ah. Am I to be pinked for dallying with young Frederick in the garden?" asked Shauna at her naughtiest,
stealing his lordship's thunder with the suggestion of a
smile.

"Then you are aware of the impropriety of your conduct," said his lordship. It was not a question, and he expected no reply. He had a ready lecture to read, but Shauna was before him with a gurgle of laughter.

"Nonsense. Impropriety, indeed!" With her chin, she indicated the house. "Look there, we sat in full view of the garden windows . . . and we talked, older woman to troubled young man. . . . Tell me, where is the impropriety?"

He shook his head and his brows were drawn. "You have a habit of turning things about, but it won't do, Shauna. Can't you see the lad is in love with you?"

"Absurd, Damien . . . " she said softly, tenderly, and then more formally, "No, my lord, not in love, infatuated. He admires me. Excellent, for then he might be directed by me, and at the moment, he needs direction."

"Which he should be getting from me," said his lordship testily.

"Yes, but it seems he wants your respect, your admiration, your approval . . . and finds himself instead falling into scrapes which he dare not confess to you, for then he thinks he would not be able to attain your . . . respect, admiration, and approval."

"Scrapes. . . ? Has he fallen into yet another scrape?" his lordship shot at her with some concern.

She looked up at him, puzzled, and then sighed, "Well, I think so, but I can't be certain. . . . We shall see."

They were almost at the house. The front doors stood only a few feet from them, and he knew an urge to touch her, did in fact take her elbow. "One wonders, Miss Shauna, how we ever managed to get on without you," he said dryly.

"Hmmm," agreed Miss Shauna. "One wonders, indeed, my lord," with which she laughed deliciously.

Chapter Twelve

Spring was now displaying itself in full array. Wildflowers lined the side of the road and permeated the air with their arresting scents. A breeze, slight but cool as it came in its soft waves, played with Shauna's black silky hair and rippled at her straw bonnet. She adjusted the ribbon at her neck with one gloved hand while she managed the matched chestnut pair before her with the other.

"Sweet-goers . . ." she commented quietly, more to herself than to the twins.

Felix sat forward in the gig and bent over his sister, who sat between him and Shauna. "Do you think so? I wanted Jeffries to hitch up the bays. Now, *they* can move!"

"I have no doubt of that, for I have seen them," laughed Shauna. "However, it would not be seemly for the Bromley governess to be driving them." Too often the twins treated her as though she were family. That was something she had to deal with carefully. They must remember her position.

Felix pooh-poohed such talk in unintelligible sounds, ending it with, "Stuff, I say. You could handle them . . . not a bit ham-handed"—he looked towards his brother, who was riding astride near enough to the gig to hear him—"like Freddy here. . . ." A wide grin spread across his impish face.

"Brat!" called Freddy, reaching down to pop him a swat with the end of his crop over his uncovered head.

Francine observed all this and suddenly hugged Shauna around the waist, sighing loudly and happily. "See . . . oh, just see how everything is perfect since you came to us. I shall never let you go, Miss Shauna. I want you with us always."

"You are very sweet. I do love being here at Bromley with you and Felix, but you know, always is not something to bank on."

Francine wrinkled her nose. "What do you mean?"

"Well, one can never predict the future. You don't know for certain what you will be doing every minute of every hour in every day. Always and never are words . . . that are very difficult to hold, but never mind, the feeling is there."

"Yes, but . . ." Francine pursued, "I don't want you to go."

"No, you don't, and I don't want to go. That should do for now."

"Yes, but . . ." Francine was not about to give up.

Shauna touched her chin. "My little love, I shall stand your friend wherever I might be, and hopefully I shall not be far when you need me."

"Females!" stuck in Felix, now thoroughly bored with the topic of conversation. "Forever going on and on about something mushy! What I want to know is, can we go to that bang-up cake shoppe for tarts and hot chocolate?"

Shauna eyed him warningly. "*Not* if you mean to stuff your little face with half a dozen of those things and ruin your dinner!"

"No, no, I promise . . . not more than five." Felix twinkled at her.

"Your brother is every bit the brat you called him, Freddy!" laughed Shauna. For no good reason a picture of Damien came to mind. Two days. It had been two long

72

days since she had seen him. He had suddenly picked himself up and advised them that he had to return to London. No further explanation had been given, and then he was gone. She had never missed anyone in quite this way. It was ridiculous, she told herself. Was this love? If so, why did it hurt so?

His lordship tooled his spirited dapple with a sure skill, but his mind was not on schooling his horse as he made his leisurely way down the Post Road back to Bromley. He had been in London for two days. Two days, only two days, and yet it seemed a century. He was itching to be back at Bromley, back overseeing the twins . . . and Shauna. This was absurd! Shauna indeed. This wayward kind of thinking had to end. He was going to be married. He had returned to London in hopes of visiting with his intended, but upon his morning call to Lady Elton he had been informed that Miss Elton was still quite unwell abovestairs. He had done the expected, sent her flowers and a note advising her that he looked for her speedy recovery.

Perhaps now marriage would not be necessary. Perhaps Miss Elton was the wrong choice. After all, she might prove to be sickly, and that would be damned inconvenient! What a tangle. Here was Shauna, seeing to the twins' education, their manners, their self-esteem, their . . . needs. Here was Shauna . . . enchanting him with her every move, with the sound of her laugh, the touch of her smile, the heat from her body . . .

Stop! Damnation, Damien, he told himself severely, just stop. Get control. You have always had control before . . . in everything. There never was a woman before who made you lose yourself. There never was Shauna before, he answered.

Bromley loomed closer in the distance, and he actually felt his heartbeat increase rapidly. Excitement tickled his nerves. He missed the twins. He actually missed them, for he had enjoyed them on this visit, but . . . something more made him thrill as he passed through Bromley Park and came closer still to the house. Shauna. Soon he would see Shauna. . . .

Shauna glanced up at the descending sun, at the gathering clouds, and consulted Freddy as they left the sweet shoppe and moved towards the livery where their carriage and horses had been left. ''Gracious, it must be getting terribly late. . . ?'' Shauna's lips pursed together as she considered the consequences of the excursion, for she expected, hoped, that Damien would be home today. Would he be angry with her for keeping the children in town after dark?

Frederick was preoccupied. He had, in fact, not been his usual merry self during the latter part of their expedition. He considered his timepiece and said absently that it was already after five o'clock.

''Faith! Well, we had better step lively then. . . .'' She noticed that Freddy was looking across the street, nodding toward an odd-looking gentleman. Shauna's fine brows drew together. The man across the way was standing in the doorway of a drinking establishment. He wore a weathered gray top hat. His face was grizzled, and his clothing shabby. Her gray eyes opened wide and flew to Freddy's face. What in heaven's name had Freddy to do with such a character?

''Shauna . . . do you think . . . I mean . . . I am sorry, but there is one more thing I *must* take care of while I am in town. Would you mind terribly if I let you start without me?''

She knew he expected her to reply in the positive, and while she really didn't mind the notion of driving unescorted, she did mind his going off with such a rough-looking individual. ''Yes, but Freddy . . . it is already getting quite dark . . . and I don't relish the notion of taking the Post Road in an open carriage alone at this hour. . . ." Zounds, she thought, that brazen man across the street was actually beckoning to Freddy!

"Forgive me, Shauna. I must leave you now . . . but I swear, I shan't be long." He squeezed her gloved hand. "I will handle this and catch up to you in a trice!" He was already in the middle of the road, and although the seedy-looking character he went to meet was grinning broadly, Freddy's countenance was grave.

Shauna watched Frederick fall into step with this man, and she watched them as they went into the drinking establishment. Well, Freddy was playing deep, but at what? There was nothing for it. She would have to start without him. She called to Francine, who was a few feet away looking in at a trimming shoppe, and Felix, who was playing at "jacks" just beside her, and some ten minutes later found them on the Post Road.

Shauna's first trip to town had been done in a most seemly fashion, but she was too pretty, too vivacious, and too amiable for it to be a quiet visit. She attracted attention, stirred curiosity, and certainly turned heads. Two of those heads belonged to the Anderson brothers.

Catching sight of her early in the afternoon, they made it their business to discover who she was. The answer to this question so startled them that they began to look her way for the remainder of the afternoon. Just what was such a young, beautiful girl doing being a governess? They eyed one another and decided this was an incredible waste. Something had to be done, but first they would have to find a way of getting to know the girl. They made the attempt, and it was both clumsy and rejected.

The Anderson boys came right up to her, and though they bowed, hats in hand, as they introduced themselves, she was both curt and cold. She thought their bold behavior disrespectful. She had never put up with such nonsense before and would not now.

The Anderson brothers were idle beings used to kicking up larks and getting through one scrape only to land in another. Their father was a wealthy mill owner who smiled fondly at their mischievousness and called such behavior "normal high spirits." Thus they reached the ages of twenty and eighteen pampered, petted, and supported throughout. Shauna had snubbed them, and Thomas, the older Anderson, advised his brother that he meant to teach her manners.

"Just who does she think she is?" asked Thomas, not expecting a reply. "She is naught but a governess. I gave her the chance to chat with *me*, Tom Anderson, and she stuck up her nose at me."

"Aw . . . didn't know who we are. New in town, you know," answered William Anderson, more inclined to keep his brother's heady temper in check.

"Well, then she wants a lesson, eh, Billy-boy?"

"What kind of lesson?" William was wary.

"Think we should follow her out on the Post Road and give her escort home?"

"She don't want it, and besides, she came in with the young lord. He will be taking her home." William didn't want any trouble with the Bromleys. Theirs was a powerful family, and more than once he had heard his father warn them off the Bromleys and his lordship Drummond.

"He won't," answered Thomas. "Saw him leave her be. . . . He went off, he did. Didn't you notice, Billy?"

"No, I didn't, but forget it, Tom. No point. She is just a female. No sense in scaring her."

"Don't mean to scare her precisely, mean to escort her home" was all that Thomas would answer. "Come on then, let's get our horses and catch up to her."

"Aw, Tom . . ." complained his brother. He couldn't see the fun in this, and he could see trouble.

His lordship, Damien, paced about the hall waiting for his family and their governess to return from town. It was nearing five o'clock and there was no sign of them. Soon it would be dark, and there had been stories about highwaymen on the Post Road. Well, there was Freddy escorting them after all. Ah yes, Freddy. He shook his head, but Freddy was really only a boy. Seventeen . . . He never carried a weapon. . . .

That was it. He would go and meet them. His own horse was too fatigued from the journey from London, but he could use the dark bay that Shauna had been riding. He hurried to the stables and helped Tom groom and tack up the bay, for he was in a rush to be off.

It was already dark, and for reasons she could not put into clear thought, Shauna felt uneasy. The twins chatted happily about their afternoon, and applied various questions to Shauna, who answered absently as she guided the team over the badly rutted road.

"There is someone riding up on us," announced Felix suddenly. He was turned halfway round and was studying the road at their backs.

"How do you know?" his sister asked anxiously. "I can't see anyone."

"I can hear a horse. . . ." Felix was frowning. ". . . And look at the dust. They are riding hard."

Shauna glanced back but had all she could do to keep her horses in hand. They were acting up, for they, too, heard something coming up swiftly behind them. "Easy, lads . . ." Shauna soothed, but they were fidgeting to move, to get away.

Two riders came upon them and boldly moved to their horses' heads, commanding, "Ho there, loves . . . ho . . ."

Shauna pulled her team up, for these riders had moved

into her path and spooked her horses. "Just what do you think you are doing?" she demanded sharply, angrily.

"Now, now, missy, calm yourself, do. . . ." grinned Thomas Anderson as he tipped his hat to her. "We came along after you to give you escort home."

"Thank you, but I don't recall asking that of you." Shauna's gray eyes flashed.

"No, so you didn't, but we did notice that the young lord wasn't with you when you left the village, and this is an open road, you know . . . dangerous."

"Dangerous?" Shauna frowned and glanced at the twins. Francine slipped her little gloved hand onto Shauna's lap for comfort as Shauna's hands were busy with the driving reins. Shauna smiled at her and returned her attention to the Andersons. "I don't see why you consider this road dangerous. . . . And we haven't far to go."

"That may be so, but as it happens, this road *is* dangerous. People have been accosted by highwaymen. . . . And what they might do if they came upon such a pretty little helpless thing such as yourself. . . ?"

"Nonsense!" Shauna returned impatiently.

"Here, love . . ." said Thomas Anderson, ". . . why not let me drive you home? My brother can take my horse along. . . ." He was already dismounting, coming for the reins, moving with every intention of taking a seat beside Shauna.

"Stop it!" ordered Shauna sharply.

"Hey . . . there isn't even room," put in Felix suddenly. "Go away!"

During this altercation, William Anderson had a time with his horse and was too busy to notice a rider bearing down upon them. Something, however, caught his eye, and he looked up to gulp. It was now quite dark, and what he saw was a large, darkly clad man, cloak flowing in the breeze, on a bay horse moving at some speed directly for

78

them. He gulped in some inexplicable fear and called his brother's attention. "Tom! Eh, Tom!"

Thomas Anderson looked round irritably, for Shauna had just taken her driving whip and threatened him with it. "What, fool?" There was no need to reply, for Lord Damien Drummond was already upon them and looking like a thunder god!

"What the devil is the meaning of this?" he demanded of Thomas Anderson, who stood still near the open carriage.

"Nothing at all. We were just offering to drive the lady and her brats home. That's all!" Thomas answered audaciously. " 'Tis none of your affair, now is it?"

"Allow me to advise you that even if the lady you refer to were not under the protection of my family because of the status she holds in our household, even if the *brats* were not my own brother and sister, still would I take exception to you forcing yourself upon them!"

"Zounds, man . . ." breathed William. "It's himself! 'Tis Lord Drummond." He turned to his lordship. "Sorry, my lord; indeed, we had no idea . . . meant no harm. . . ."

"Is that so?" His lordship directed his question to Thomas, still standing beside the carriage.

Thomas was defiant but not stupid. He lowered his gaze and mumbled, "No harm intended." So saying, he climbed into his saddle and, without looking back, took off toward town. His brother cursed beneath his breath and followed.

"Are you alright?" his lordship asked Shauna softly.

She smiled at him. "Yes, thank you. I don't think they meant more than to force their attentions upon . . . us. . . ."

"Ay," agreed Felix, "but Shauna was going to bash him over the head with the whip!" He was beaming. "She is a right 'un."

"We will talk about this later." He cast his eyes round as though looking for someone and asked, his brows drawn, "And where is Freddy? I was told he had gone in with you today to the village."

"Yes, yes . . . Freddy gave us escort and meant to catch up to us. . . . I . . . I suppose he was delayed." Shauna looked away. She didn't want Freddy to catch a lecture and therefore did not wish to say anything further on the subject.

"Delayed? Really? He allowed you to set off on the Post Road at this hour . . . alone?" Clearly his lordship was astonished. He could not believe that Freddy would have been so lost to all the proprieties that he could have allowed any female, let alone the one he was infatuated with, to drive alone with the twins on an open road in an open carriage after dark.

"Well, it was not quite dark when we set out. . . ." Shauna said meekly.

"Indeed. Drive on, Miss Shauna. I am certain the household anxiously awaits our return."

As "household" could only mean staff, and since his lordship had never indicated any concern for the staff's interests in their regard, she found this a remarkable statement. However, she made no demur as she urged the fidgety pair forward.

Little was said on the drive homeward, for even the twins were strangely reticent. As it happened, Felix was thinking about his brother Freddy. He had experienced a lesson and was slowly absorbing it. Damien had indicated disapprobation for Freddy's neglect. Felix adored Freddy. However, he had seen that this time a breaking with the rules had put Miss Shauna into an uncomfortable situation. This was something to think about.

Francine had been silent throughout the encounter and her brother's timely arrival on the scene. Quietly she leaned against Felix and said, "Freddy is in for it. . . . And this time, Felix, I rather think he deserves a good dressing down.''

''Ay,'' grumbled Felix, ''maybe . . . I dunno . . . don't want to talk about it.''

Wisely Francine kept still and looked instead from Damien to Miss Shauna. He didn't seem to like her. She couldn't understand why. She puzzled over the problem, for it was not Miss's fault that they had been bothered by those dreadful men. Yet here was Damien very nearly steaming, and he had the look about him that boded ill for everyone!

Chapter Thirteen

Dinner had been consumed in a strained atmosphere of virtual silence. Freddy was not yet home. The fact hovered over them like an ominous cloud. The twins complained that they were fatigued and retired to their rooms as soon as they had swallowed their dessert.

Damien took up his snifter of brandy from the sideboard and glanced at Shauna, who softly said that she, too, meant to retire to her room with a book.

"No"—he moved toward her—"wait awhile yet. There is a splendid fire lit in the library, where I have requested they bring your coffee. I have noticed that you enjoy a cup after your dinner." He smiled with all the charm he was noted for. "Please."

She hesitated, but then replied, "Very well, if you like." She sincerely had wished to avoid any discussion about Freddy, and she had no doubt that this was why Damien wanted her company in the library.

"Indeed, I would like that very much," he answered, and opened the door of the dining room to allow her to pass.

In the library they did find a pleasant fire and the lighting seemed quietly inviting. Shauna felt oddly shy as she moved about the room in an effort to find a comfortable position. Finally she decided on the high-backed winged chair closest to the fire.

He watched her, and something inside of him was excitingly vibrating. What? His heart? Absurd. It was desire, nothing more. He went to sit on the brown velvet sofa across from her and took a sip of his brandy before saying, "I am pleased with the progress you have made with Felix and Francine. They appear to be . . . coming out of their shells."

She looked at him for a long moment and smiled warmly. "Thank you."

The library door was opened and the butler came in quietly and set a tray down before Shauna on a small table. He poured her a cup of coffee, put a dab of cream in it as she liked, and asked if there would be anything else that would be needed. His lordship thanked him, and he withdrew from the room wondering what Lord Drummond was at entertaining a governess in this fashion.

Shauna laughed after the butler had gone and said, "He does not approve."

"Does he not?" His lordship was grinning. "Well, it is not his place to approve or disapprove of anything I might do."

"And what of me?" Her brow was up with a challenge, but there was a twinkle in her gray eyes.

"You are in my employ. You have little choice."

"Oh, I don't know. You couldn't make me stay here alone in this room with you if I did not wish to," she answered saucily.

"But you do wish to. . . ." It was most charmingly said.

"The rogue in me does, yes," she admitted freely, and diverted him by looking away as she sipped her coffee. "Hmmm. This is good."

"But the governess in you does not," he said, and smiled softly at her. Before she could answer he went on,

"Shauna . . . there is something about you that intrigues me."

"Is that a compliment?" she giggled.

"Of course, but what I mean precisely is . . . I would like to know about the circumstances that brought you to this pass."

She blushed, because she didn't want to tell him an outright lie. "I would rather not discuss my personal affairs. You have said that you are pleased with my work as the twins' governess. Is that not enough?"

He got up and started to pace. When he turned he looked at her long. "No. It is not enough. Look at you! Look at the way you carry yourself, the way you ride . . . even your clothes. You have certainly chosen two quiet, orderly gowns for your wardrobe, but I'd wager a monkey they come from the best shop on Bond Street!"

"So they do. I was taken care of until my family chose to do otherwise . . . for reasons I do not wish to discuss," she answered briefly.

"They threw you out? I don't believe it!"

"No, they did not. They made it impossible for me to stay. Remember . . . it was I . . . running away. . . ."

"This is absurd. Are you trying to tell me that you need not be a governess to earn your keep?"

"I am telling you that I choose to be a governess to your darling Felix and Francine," she answered, her brow up. She put down her cup of coffee and moved up and away from her chair towards the library door.

He was on her in a trice, holding her arm. He turned her round to him and huskily, tenderly said her name. "Shauna . . ." His lips took hers, gently at first. Then, feeling her excitement, he parted her lips to tease her mouth with his tongue.

She pulled away. "Please, my lord . . . do not."

"I want you. . . . I could take care of you. . . ." he said hungrily.

She knew his meaning and her brow went up, gray eyes glinted. "So . . . I should take on two responsibilities. The twins' schoolroom by day, your bedroom by night? I think not." She did move away then, and she did not look back. It was a good thing, for there was a smile just lurking about her pretty mouth. She wasn't displeased, not in the slightest! She would have him propose one day, even though he thought her a governess. Faith, she hoped she could accomplish such a feat, for she loved him. Oh, how she loved him!

Chapter Fourteen

They sat in a sombre mood at the breakfast table. The day was a bright one and spring was displaying itself in seductive waves, but even this did not heighten the spirits of the assembled family at Bromley. This was due totally to the fact that Freddy had not returned home until twenty minutes before breakfast was served!

He attempted a cavalier air as he sauntered past his older half brother and made for his bedroom.

"Frederick!" His lordship's tone boded trouble.

"Hallo. See you later, Damien. Mean to get some sleep and be down for lunch." Freddy was dying on the inside and unable to meet Damien's glaring blue eyes.

"I don't mean to cast a rub in your plans, but I fear I must. Come with me to the library."

They went off together, the exchange witnessed by the twins and their governess, who had stopped short at the top of the stairs in time to catch the last of the conversation. Felix and Francine eyed one another and then turned up their eyes to Shauna. She raised hers heavenward and commented, "Perhaps this is not the moment to ask your brother for permission to visit the Wilsons."

"Aw . . ." started Felix.

"Hmmm," agreed Francine, "he would only say no.

Didn't you see his face, Felix? He is very angry with Freddy.''

"Awww . . ." was all the comment Felix meant to make on the subject. He turned around and went back to the schoolroom.

Shauna smiled at Francine. "We might as well do lessons now, and then perhaps we can visit the Wilsons in the afternoon. Would you like that?''

"Which?'' peeped Francine. "Doing lessons now or visiting the Wilsons later?''

"Never mind, puss . . . off you go.'' Shauna was smiling fondly, but her mind was on Freddy and Damien. She hoped Damien was handling things correctly, for she rather guessed that Freddy was in deep waters and needed help. He certainly would not ask for it if Damien was dressing him down too harshly.

That had been before they had all sat down to breakfast. What had been discussed, Shauna could only guess. The outcome, however, was something she was fairly certain was dreadfully at odds with what either Damien or Freddy wanted. Damien ate his meal in cold silence, and Freddy ate very little. Shauna sighed out loud and drew Damien's hard blue eyes.

"Is there something amiss with your meal, Miss Shauna?'' His brow was up, and clearly it was a reprimand.

She twinkled at him. "The coffee is lovely and the cinnamon toast quite perfect, thank you.''

"Humph,'' returned his lordship. "You don't eat enough, and I have noticed that you have taken off too much weight since you first arrived at Bromley.''

"I eat quite enough, thank you,'' replied Shauna, smiling sweetly.

He grimaced at her but said no more on the subject. She saw that the twins had finished their meals and were fidgeting to be off. She lowered her lashes and asked his lordship softly, "May I take the twins and retire to the schoolroom?"

He nodded, allowed Francine to run to him and kiss his cheek, smiled at Felix, and then he and Freddy stood as Shauna took her charges and left them be.

Freddy did not sit back down but looked frostily at his older brother and said, "Must I also request permission to be excused, my lord brother?"

"You are a man, are you not? You decide what you must and must not do, what is right . . . what is not," Damien said on a frown.

Freddy strode from the room, and though he dearly wanted to slam the door at his back, he restrained himself. On the other side he saw Shauna, for she turned round at the bottom of the stairs and looked his way. To the twins she said hurriedly, "Better go up . . . quickly. I shall join you two in a moment . . . for I dearly want to speak to Freddy."

"Good idea!" declared Francine, and took her brother's arm to drag him up the stairs.

"I want to listen," declared Felix, but allowed his sister to pull him along.

Shauna went to Freddy and said, "Shall we talk?"

He shook his head. "It is . . . more than I can bear. . . . I am so very ashamed."

"What do you mean?"

"Damien told me that you were accosted on the road. Shauna . . . I feel a cad. . . ."

"Absurd boy!" she answered him at once, and took his hand. "Come into the library and we will sort things out. I am a very good listener . . . as well as a good talker, and you need to have a little of both."

He went with her and plopped himself down heavily on the sofa as she sat beside him. He leaned forward with his elbows on his knees and his head in his hands. "I have made such a mull of it . . . and what you must think me. . . ?''

"What I think is that you have been playing deep and need a hand to help you out of the mire. All of us do from time to time, you know.''

He looked at her sharply and breathed on a whisper, "You don't know how deep. . . . And there is no help for it now.''

"There is always help, though we don't always recognize it. Come then, Freddy . . . what is it? Gotten yourself into debt?'' It was a guess, but one based on many small things that Shauna had noticed in the last two weeks.

"How . . . how could you know . . . ?'' he was startled into replying.

"Never mind that. How much do you owe, Freddy?'' she pursued on a gentle note.

"More than I was able to pay . . . and it was a debt of honor.'' His voice dropped an octave. "I had no choice. . . . I had to pay it.''

"A gambling debt? Oh, Freddy . . . I see,'' she returned sympathetically. No point in dressing him down for gambling a sum he had no means of paying. That was done. "Then . . . the debt is still outstanding? Is that it?''

"No. I paid it. . . . I went to a . . . a moneylender.'' He hung his head.

"You what?'' she was shocked into almost shrieking. "Never say he loaned you money? You are underage!''

"I don't know about that. . . . He didn't seem to care about my age. Knew I was Lord Bromley and that one day . . . Well, never mind all that. I had to put up m'father's ring. It is an old emerald—they used to wear those ornate things back in the 1770's—and it was passed on to him by his father. I don't wear it, but I keep it, you see. . . . And I am sick about it, Shauna, so you needn't look at me like that.''

"How much did you owe, Freddy?'' she asked quietly.

"You don't want to know." He looked away.

"Oh, but I do. How much, Freddy?"

"A thousand pounds." Again he looked away.

Shauna swallowed the words that sprang to her lips. She took a minute to compose herself and asked, "And of course you did not confide in your brother?"

"No . . . how can I? He already thinks me so irresponsible. . . ." His voice trailed away.

"I shan't go into that. There is no point in dwelling on how it happened. It did. Now we must set it right. You must tell Damien. Come clean. He will be angry, but he will think more of you for confessing the whole."

"No."

"Freddy, trust me. Allow your brother . . . to be a brother to you."

The library door opened and Damien stood there, his face a mask.

"Do I intrude?" he asked on a dry note.

Shauna could have boxed his ears. Inwardly she fumed and marveled at his ill timing. Instead of gritting her teeth, however, she smiled sweetly and said, "Why, how so? You could not intrude in your own home."

"It isn't *his* home," Freddy stuck in pugnaciously, "it is *my* home. This is Bromley Grange, not Drummond Towers!"

Shauna rounded on Freddy like a tigress. "What an unhandsome thing to say. His lordship is not only your guardian, but your brother as well."

Freddy flushed and immediately retracted. "I am sorry, Damien."

Damien was frowning to himself. Clearly he had gone very wrong with Freddy. He had only succeeded in alienating him. He loved Freddy, and he had hoped that would show through the lectures he had been putting to the lad. Obviously, he had handled things in a clumsy fashion.

What to do? He answered quietly, "I know, Freddy. . . . Don't think of it."

Shauna got to her feet. "Well, I have dallied with you long enough, Frederick. The twins are probably tearing the schoolroom apart by now." She started for the door. Damien reached for and touched her arm as she passed him, and she stopped.

"Shauna"—his voice was gentle—"you needn't go."

She smiled at him. "Oh, I think I must." On a softer note she added, " 'Tis time for brothers . . . to be just that."

He watched her leave. What an unusual girl she was, so very full of wisdom. He turned to Freddy. Indeed, it was time he approached the situation from a different point of view.

Chapter Fifteen

Lady Elton paced. She eyed the letter she clasped in her hand and then she plopped herself down in her pink satin lady's chair to read it again.

Dearest Lady Elton:

In reply to your very welcome letter, I regret to advise you that Shauna is not with me.

It grieves me to read that you have been ill with worry.

At least I may rest your fears and assure you that Shauna is safe and, I believe, happy.

I can not divulge her whereabouts, for I gave her my word that I would not. Forgive me.

I will, however, forward your letter to her so that she may see for herself what suffering you are experiencing. Perhaps then she may reconsider and return home.

Fondly,
Polly Corbett

Well, what was she to do now? Naught. Polly Corbett was her last hope. There was something in this, though. At least Shauna had been in touch with Polly. At least Shauna was safely installed somewhere. Yes, but where?

Her bedroom door opened and her maid bobbed a curtsey, saying, "His lordship of Dartford be here, m'lady, and he says to tell ye he won't be put off today."

"Kit! Good gracious. What shall I tell him?" Lady Elton stood up and nearly wailed.

"Mayhap the truth, m'lady. Miss Shauna and his lordship were ever good friends. He jest might be knowing where she could be. . . ."

"Hush, you dreadful child! You and Shauna were good friends. Do you know where she is?"

"No, I've told ye . . . and told ye. If I knew, I would tell ye fer her sake, fer yer sake . . . but I don't."

"Yes, yes. Very well then . . . perhaps I should take someone into my confidence. . . . Perhaps young Dartford might be able to help." She moved to her mirror, saying over her shoulder, "Show his lordship to the library, and have coffee brought to us there."

"Yes, m'lady."

Lady Elton patted her short gray curls, screwed up her mouth, shook her head, and bolstered herself. Kit Dartford was a friend. He could be trusted . . . of course he could.

Kit Dartford was, like Shauna, one and twenty years old. He was tall, lean, athletically built, and quite boyishly attractive. His hair was layered in waves of gold to his neckline, and his eyes were an interesting shade of green. He was considered to be a marriage prize and was much sought after even though he was only just out of Eton. He, however, had little interest in women or marriage. His great passions were fox hunting, foxhounds, and field hunters!

His and Shauna's friendship had started when they toddled across to one another in the presence of their laughing parents. Since that time their friendship was of such a nature that time and even the separation brought about by their divergent life-styles could not alter their easy comradeship. They always seemed to gravitate toward one another. It had been some weeks since he had seen Shauna, as he had been in the country visiting friends. Upon being told that she was ill when he had come by some days before, he had demanded to be taken to her room. They had refused his request, stating that she might be infectious. He had grumbled, but he had gone away. Now he would not take no for an answer. "See her I will, infectious be damned!" he advised Lady Elton's maid.

Lady Elton entered the library and went forward, her hands outstretched to clasp Kit's.

"Darling . . . how lovely to see you. . . ." She took and squeezed his hands.

"What's this about my Shauna?" He was always direct and rarely bothered with amenities.

"Sit, my dear . . . we must talk," said Lady Elton gravely.

Kit was startled into speechlessness. Could Shauna be in a bad way? Hell! Was she dying? He sat, because the fear of this suddenly hit him.

"There . . ." offered Lady Elton, patting his knee, "don't look like that, Kit. You see . . . I have something to tell you, but it may not be repeated. . . . You must give me your word."

"My word? Of course, on my honor! Now, what is wrong with Shauna?"

"She has run away. . . ." Lady Elton dove right in on a hushed note.

"She what?" It was nearly a shout of laughter. "Upon my soul! The little devil. Whatever possessed her to do that?"

"I am afraid . . . it is all my fault. You see . . . she got herself into a dreadful scrape. . . . Oh, Kit . . . you can't imagine. . . ."

"Oh yes I can. Besides, the Jersey told me all about it. Said if she didn't curb herself and her wayward ways, she would be refused vouchers to Almack's."

"Well . . . precisely. She was so very restless and getting wilder by the day . . . but never mind. Lord Drummond offered for her, you see. . . ."

"Lord Drummond?" Kit was moved to ejaculate, "Upon my soul!"

"Just so." Her ladyship was pleased to find Kit's ready understanding. "What was I to do? Let such a catch slip away? I agreed."

"Without Shauna's consent?" Kit nearly whooped with surprise. "Never say so! She wouldn't have him . . . not unless she wanted him, and how could she? . . . Pretty sure she didn't have the foggiest notion who he was."

"As you say, she wouldn't have him. Said a great deal about not marrying unless it was for love . . . and thought me . . . a . . . a stepmother. . . ."

"Well, you are her stepmother," said Kit reasonably.

"Yes, but she said I was no better than . . . a typical stepmother," returned Lady Elton, still smarting from the accusation.

"No . . . not typical . . . not you . . . not Shauna . . . not the situation. So she balked. . . . But that doesn't mean a thing. Don't signify. She doesn't want him . . . doesn't have to have him. Why run away?"

"Told her that she had no choice. I would make her marry him."

"You never did that?" Kit was amazed.

"I did . . . and I think I meant it. . . . At any rate, Shauna believed I meant it. Took off in the middle of the night . . . weeks ago, and I can't find her."

"Hmmm. Polly, you know. Went to Polly, I'd wager," said Kit after just a moment's thought.

"Polly writes that Shauna isn't with her. . . ."

"Does she? Never mind that. Polly wouldn't rat on Shauna. . . . But that's where she is. Has to be. I'll go fetch her."

"Will you?" Lady Elton's face lit up.

"Ay. I'll bring her home, see if I don't."

"Oh, Kit. You are a dear, for I don't know what I was going to tell his lordship. . . He is bound to be calling again soon."

"Did she object to Drummond . . . think him too old. . . ?" Kit asked on a frown.

"That's the other thing. Never even had a chance to tell her who had offered for her. . . ."

"You mean she doesn't know it's Drummond himself?" Kit was incredulous.

"She didn't care . . . said she wasn't in love and wouldn't marry anyone without love."

"Loon of a girl . . . but the best there is. I'll fetch her home. Tell her she don't have to marry anyone she doesn't want."

"Oh, Kit . . . can't you try and talk her into marrying Drummond? I . . . I do think it would be so good for her. . . ."

"No," said Kit emphatically. "Don't fret though, Lady Elton, Shauna will do . . . always has. Knows her mind, she does."

"Yes, but—"

"Well, I'm off." Kit was already making for the door. Another adventure! There now, wasn't it just like Shauna to be thrusting them both into adventure!

Chapter Sixteen

Shauna had watched Damien and Freddy leave together and she had bit her lip. They had both looked so gravely serious, so determined. What had passed between them in the library? Where were they going? What was going on, and why weren't they home yet? It was nearly time for tea.

The twins came skipping into the library and plopped themselves in front of the fireplace, where Francine hugged her knees to her chin and announced that she was famished.

"Ay," agreed Felix, "do we have to wait for Damien and Freddy? Can't we have tea brought in, Miss Shauna?"

Shauna moved to the large window overlooking the drive and nearly clapped her hands. "Here they are now! Are you all washed, you two?" She noticed both men were looking a great deal happier than when they had left. Damien was in fact rubbing his hands together and then taking up Freddy's arm as he took the steps to the front doors. There, they would be in any minute. She moved to the bellrope and rang it for tea.

Freddy strode into the library a moment later, but Damien was not there. Shauna looked past him and frowned. She tried to stop herself from asking but only succeeded in tempering her tone. "Isn't his lordship coming in for tea. . . ?"

"Damien? Ay," answered Freddy in good spirits, "he'll be here in a moment. Had a letter waiting for him. . . ." He moved toward the twins. "Hallo, brats. Did you miss me?"

Francine jumped up and threw her arms round his neck as he bent to kiss her cheek. He ruffled Felix's hair, and Felix grunted something brotherly and quite incoherent. Shauna smiled.

"Is everything . . . better, Freddy?" She eyed him penetratingly.

"I have been a fool, Shauna. Damien is the best of great brothers, and I mean to take care I shan't be any trouble in the future. Does that answer your question?"

"Oh yes, Freddy, I am so pleased."

Damien strode into the room and Shauna felt herself riveted. She couldn't look away from him. He was so tall, so handsome, so well formed, and his eyes . . . so blue. They twinkled at her now.

"Well . . . I rather thought you would have had tea warmed and ready for us. . . ."

No sooner uttered but a male servant appeared with the tea cart fully laden with delectables. Freddy made a move in its direction, as did Felix, who declared happily, "Tarts! Strawberry tarts!"

It was some hours afterwards, long after dinner and a game of ducks and drakes, that Shauna announced her intention of seeing the twins to bed. Felix groaned and said he wanted to play another game. Francine sighed and said she didn't, for she was sleepy. Damien chuckled and said, "Come on, I'll take you up. . . ."

Freddy got to his feet and forestalled him. "No, allow me, Damien. I haven't had the treat in a long time. . . .

Besides, I just remembered a story I don't think they have heard." He looked in their direction. "What say you?"

The children echoed their approval in hearty accents, and both Shauna and Damien watched their departure in some amusement. Shauna peeped at Damien and remarked, "I don't know what you two talked about . . . or what you did, but whatever it was, it has had a profound effect on Freddy. Why, I thought I would die when he announced his intentions of picking up his books and studying tomorrow. Says he means to make up the work he has missed and get himself reinstated at school!"

Damien was on his feet, putting down his snifter of brandy, walking towards her. He didn't want to speak, but he didn't stop her from rattling on about dinner, about the twins, until she stopped and looked deep into his intense blue eyes. Still, he didn't say a word as he put out his hands and waited for her to place her own in his. She did. She didn't know why she did, she only knew she couldn't stop herself. He helped her to her feet.

It was inevitable that the moment would take them into the next, which was filled with electricity. It ran through him to her and then back again to him as his arms wrapped around her body, as his mouth parted her lips, as his tongue searched out her own.

She couldn't stop her response, and her response was to hold to him, press herself to him. His kiss moved into another and she felt the room spin as her knees weakened. He held her tight, he held her up. Shauna, she heard herself think, get control, stop, Shauna, stop!

She managed to put up her hand and push against his chest. He allowed her to pull away because there were words he wanted to say, so many words playing in his mind, fighting with his heart. What he said was "I want you, sweetheart. . . . Come upstairs. . . ."

It was like a slap, cold and hard; she felt it shake her

entire being, but quickly she recovered. Softly, sadly she answered, "No. I don't think so."

He frowned down at her and his hands dropped to his side. "Yes, of course, don't tell me. Your morals dictate otherwise."

"An answer, but not mine."

"No? Then what answer is there?"

"Oh, my lord, you must know." She was smiling at him, though she was trembling from the effort.

"I do not." He was testy. He wanted her. It was all he was prepared to understand at the moment. He didn't want philosophy, he wanted her in his arms, in his bed.

"You want me. As it happens . . . I rather think I want you. Perhaps we can arrange it, my lord. . . . Perhaps we can come to terms." She was playing her game but not quite enjoying it.

His brow went up. "Do you know, Shauna . . . I did not think you would sell yourself."

"Did you not? Then what were you doing just a moment ago? If I were in a position to receive an offer from you, I suppose I could have thought you were courting me. Since that is not the case, I must assume your proposition was just that. . . . And I would like to know what I may expect. I am"—and in spite of her determination, she blushed—"a virgin and therefore perhaps unschooled in the pleasures you might wish to indulge in. You should know that before you bargain with me. . . ."

"Stop it, Shauna!" He was incensed. He couldn't say why, but he was irrationally angry.

"Very well . . . " She started to move away from him, turned and eyed him meaningfully. "Then so must you."

He went towards her again, not yet willing to let her go.

"Shauna . . . there is so much we could have together . . . and I would always see to it that you are protected.

You would be under my protection. . . . Do you understand?"

Her gray eyes blazed, but she maintained her calm exterior. "I understand you very well, my lord, but you see, perhaps you don't understand me. Am I to forgo my duties as governess to the twins? I don't see how you can install me as your mistress and their governess."

He frowned and paced away from her. "Why do you have to speak about it like that?"

"How then, my lord, shall I speak of it?"

"Don't speak of it at all!" he demanded as he once again came to her and scooped her to him.

She allowed his kiss, though this time she had a touch more control of herself and did not yield to his passion. She wanted to, faith, with all her heart she wanted to, but she wanted more than he was offering, and that gave her strength. Gently she pulled out of his embrace and sweetly she looked up at him and smiled. "Dear Damien . . . I have this lamentable desire to have your arms around me . . . but I am afraid that I cannot be both your mistress and governess to the twins."

He dropped his arms and drew in a breath before releasing it slowly. "I see."

"Good," she answered promptly, and then, "If you will excuse me then, my lord . . ."

She moved to the library door, where he halted her with "Shauna!"

She turned and cocked her head. "Y-es?"

He found her irresistible, but what was he to do? She was right. It would be unforgivable of him to take her from the twins, and he could not make her his mistress while she was caring for them. Hell and fire! What was he to do? "Nothing . . . go on then . . . go to your room."

She inclined her head and left him to his thoughts. As she took the steps, she smiled to herself. Things were certainly moving along. There was a hitch, and she did not yet know how she was to manage it, but things were at least moving along.

Sleep did not come easily. Damien tossed, turned, sat up, walked about his room, stood by his window, and thought of nothing but Shauna. The gray sparkle of her eyes, the provocative curves of her body, the sensuous shape of her full lips, but it was more than her looks. There was something about the way she moved that always caught his attention. There was something about her giggle that always made him smile. There was certainly something about her . . . about all of her that made him want her desperately, more than he had ever wanted a woman before. It was insane. She was a governess. Her station in life was lower than his own . . . yes, but not her breeding. Her speech was refined, her address carefree and self-assured with the hint of sophistication, the kind that comes naturally. One might almost assume she was used to traveling amongst the beau monde.

What to do? Let it go. Let her go. He couldn't seduce the governess of his young brother and sister. That was unthinkable, yet it was what he had been thinking for weeks now. There was of course only one answer. Go to London. That's right. He would leave for London, get some perspective on this thing . . . visit his Elton bride. Right then; having made this decision, he still did not doze off until the early hours. When he awoke, it was with a start. He rushed through his morning coffee, bathed, dressed, and hurried to the stables. He was going to see to his horses himself, as he did not wish to wait around the house and bump into Shauna. He did not want to see Shauna now. What he wanted was some distance!

Chapter Seventeen

Polly Corbett—now Polly Tully—heard the sound of a horse's hooves on pebbles and moved to her lead-paned kitchen window. "Now, who can that be. . . ?" she asked her husband.

He smiled indulgently and sipped his coffee, totally aware that she did not expect him to reply to her query. He did, however, take a moment from his morning *Chronicle* to look up at the window, for indeed a swirl of dust caught his attention.

"Mercy . . . if it isn't Lord Dartford! Harry . . . 'tis Kit. . . . Oh no . . . what shall I do?" She was already adjusting her mobcap on her gray curls, rushing her hands over her full apron.

"Come to see you, has he?" was her husband's reply to her panic.

"Yes, yes . . . what else can he be doing here? He will want to know about Shauna. . . ." She was pacing.

"Will he? Well then, 'tis time," answered her husband.

"No, no . . . I promised her. . . . I can't break a promise," wailed Polly.

A knock sounded at the kitchen door, and Polly moved to open it wide and drop a curtsey. "My lord . . ." she started formally.

"My lord be hanged!" responded Kit, throwing his arms around her and planting a kiss upon her plump cheek.

She blushed and pulled away, indicating her husband. Introductions were made and an explanation started when Kit interrupted her with "Zounds, woman, you were wont to call me 'scamp, brat, whippersnapper.' Why so formal now?"

"Absurd boy!" she laughed. "Sit down and have a cup of coffee with us."

"Ah, that's more like it." He smiled and took up a chair to straddle it. He took a moment to eye her and then her elderly husband before saying, "I suppose you know why I am here?"

Polly sat down, sliding a cup towards him, not meeting his eyes.

"Yes, I suppose I do."

"Well then. Give over, do, and we'll fetch the monkey home safe and sound."

"I can't do that." Polly's hands went to her lap and she lowered her lashes. Her husband turned the page of his newspaper.

"Can't you? Why not?" Kit was surprised into asking.

"I gave her my word," returned Polly quietly.

"Silly thing to do considering what she was doing," chided Kit unmercifully but still in good spirits. "Can't set her loose in the world and then let her be. By now she no doubt wants to come home and needs to find a way."

"What do you mean?" Polly opened her eyes wide.

"Well, can't come home if she thinks her stepmama is going to marry her off to a stranger, so she holds out. Fine, but she must want to come home to her friends, her parties . . . the life she enjoys. Needs me to fetch her."

"But then she will have to marry that man . . . the one she ran away from."

"No. We'll fix that right and tight, see if we don't,"

answered Kit, beginning to grow impatient. "So tell me where she is."

"I can't. I gave her my word." Polly could be stubborn even in the face of logic.

"Polly, love . . . Shauna has to come home. She will end in kicking up the devil of a scandal if word gets out that she has run off alone, and then when she wants to come home, she won't be able to. Do you understand?"

Polly wrung her hands together. "Oh dear, oh dear."

"Precisely. So where the blazes did she go off to?"

"I am sorry, Polly dearest," her husband interjected suddenly. "You gave your word. . . . I did not." He turned to Kit. "The young lady in question is serving as governess at Bromley Grange."

"Upon my soul!" breathed Kit.

Felix was scrambling over the paddock fence and calling to his pony, Spike, who took one look at his young master and ran to the far side of the field. Surprised and irritated, Felix turned to his assembled group and shouted, "Do you see? He is being a beast!"

"Get him, Felix!" Francine encouraged as she went forward to head the pony off in Felix's direction.

Shauna smiled, folded her arms across her middle, and said to Freddy, who was standing beside her, "Perhaps a small bucket of grain will do?"

"Ay," laughed Freddy, "I'll go fetch it and be back in a minute."

"Come here, Spike . . . come on then. . . ." coaxed Francine as she put her arms up at her sides. "Go on then, Felix . . . move in. . . ."

Spike eyed him thoughtfully, looked at Francine, threw his head, and charged between them.

"Drat you, old miserable goat!" Felix called after him in disgust. "I'll get you, and when I do . . . you will be good and sorry!"

"Don't tell him that," cautioned Francine. "Then we'll never catch him."

Felix went on grumbling for some time on the infidelity of the breed when Shauna laughed and ruffled his head. "Come on then, sport, what do you expect? Here he is grazing on green grass, free to do as he pleases, and he knows if he lets you catch him, he'll have to work. He is smart."

Felix inclined his head proudly. "Ay, he is smart. But Damien says that we feed them and care for them, and in return they must give us some effort."

"Damien is quite right," agreed Shauna, thinking, Damien, oh Damien. He had left early that morning before she had a chance to see him. She had been sadly disappointed, for she had been looking forward to another encounter with him. He had left word that he was off for London and did not know when he would return.

"Here!" called Freddy, arriving with the grain. "Watch him change his tune, Felix."

Spike saw the bucket and stood still. Freddy shook the contents to tempt him further. Felix dipped his hand in and took some grain in his palm. "Look, Spike . . ."

Spike trotted right over and nibbled from Felix's hand, allowing himself to be hooked to the lead line. Francine laughed and threw her arms around him. "Silly old thing. Now you're caught."

Shauna turned her head. She heard the sound of a horse on the drive. Could it be Damien? No . . . Damien had gone off in his phaeton. Who then? Faith, but the rider looked oddly familiar, though she did not recognize the horse. Goodness, but . . . the rider seemed incredibly familiar as he drew closer. "Fire and brimstone!" Shauna snapped out loud, drawing Freddy's attention.

"What? What is it, Shauna?"

Zounds, thought Shauna, here was Kit! What was she going to do? Polly . . . oh Polly, how could you have broken your word? It couldn't be; Polly would never betray her, yet here was Kit!

Kit rode right up to them, jumped off his horse, and with reins in hand, strode up to Shauna and scooped her up with one arm. "Shauna, you brat!"

Very much to Freddy's surprise, Shauna sank into that embrace and happily responded to this greeting. "Oh, Kit . . . you dreadful man, I am so pleased to see you, even though you have no right to be here, and I am very, very upset with Polly!"

"Hush, girl! Polly did not give you away; her new husband did. Here now, go along, gather up your things and I will take you home."

She pulled away from him and stamped her foot. "Indeed, I will not!"

"Hold a moment!" stuck in Freddy, now feeling his jurisdiction. "Miss Shauna is not going anywhere."

"Is she not?" challenged Kit, a fire lighting in his green eyes. "Well, we shall see about that." To Shauna, "It's no good, old girl. You have got to come home."

"I can't, Kit. . . . Don't you understand? Stepmama wants me to marry a man I have never even seen. I don't even know his name . . . and she is adamant. She gave him her word, made a marriage settlement, means to post the banns. I won't marry a man I don't love."

"Good God, Shauna . . ." breathed Freddy, "don't you worry. No one shall take you from Bromley and force you into a marriage you don't want. You are under Bromley protection!" With which he glared defiantly at Kit, who was a good four inches taller than he.

Kit smiled. "Good boy!" He winked at Shauna. "Plucky, ain't he? Well, you have a friend in him, but tell him, do, that you have a friend in me as well."

"How can I when you have come to fetch me to . . . to a fate worse than—"

"Shauna! Don't go melodramatic and missy on me,"

107

cried Kit with a whoop of laughter. "I know you too well, and I haven't come to fetch you anywhere but home. I shan't let anyone, not even Lady Elton, marry you off. You have my word of honor."

"Shauna . . . who is this person?" demanded Freddy. "Why should we bandy words with him? Shall I send him off?"

Shauna peeped, "You deserve that, Kit, for coming here and *not* minding your own business." She turned to Freddy and said gently, "This is Lord Christopher Dartford and he is one of my dearest friends . . . very nearly like a brother." To Kit she said, "And this is Lord Frederick Bromley; playing in the paddock with the pony are the Bromley twins, Felix and Francine. I am their governess and very happy to have the position."

"So it is true. When Polly's husband told me I could scarcely credit it, and Polly would not confirm it. Said she had nothing to say on the subject. Famous! Damn, if you aren't up to every rig, you sly vixen," said Kit on an admiring note.

"I don't think he should speak to you like that," said Freddy. "Shall I land him a facer?"

"No, no, Freddy," laughed Shauna. "He really is a good sort. His want of conduct stems from the fact that we have known one another forever." She eyed Kit mischievously. "You might as well leave, for I shan't come home, and that is final."

"Yes, but, Shauna, you must," returned Kit.

"No, I must not. The twins need me, and I don't want to leave them just yet. Besides, whoever it is that I am supposed to marry will get tired of courting someone who isn't there . . . and will have to give up. Then I can come home and be comfortable."

"No, no, he thinks you are ill," returned Kit impatiently.

"Does he? Then why does he want to marry me?"

"Stupid girl. Your mama set it about that you took ill and are abovestairs. He has been fooled up to now with the rest of the world, but soon they will wonder just what it is you have contracted. Think of the scandal."

"I see. Well, it can't be helped. You go home and tell my stepmama, with whom I am still very angry, that she must remove herself to the country, where I will recover quietly without visitors. That will buy her more time."

"Selfish brat. How can you do that to her?" Kit responded sharply.

"She started it. She tried to marry me off."

"Yes, well, she is sorry for it; in a way, that is. Thought she was doing a very good thing for you."

"Well . . . perhaps I shall forgive her, but first I have something I mean to accomplish. Now, go home, Kit."

"Shall I throw him off the premises now, Shauna?" This from Freddy, who understood very little, but enough to know that in some manner this Dartford might be able to persuade Shauna to leave them. This he would not allow.

"No. We shall take him in for tea instead," laughed Shauna. "And by the way, whenever did you get that exquisite chestnut? He is prime blood!"

"Isn't he, though. Picked him up in Northumberland last month. That's what took me so long getting back to London. I was bringing him along slowly. See, while I was out attending to business, you were raking up scrapes all over town and then vanishing in the middle of the night. Need some taming, you do, Shauna my girl."

"Do I? Perhaps I just need purpose."

"And have you that here?" he asked, his brow up.

"Perhaps . . ."

Chapter Eighteen

Since Kit could not budge Shauna from her resolve to stay at Bromley, he installed himself in a local inn no more than ten minutes' ride from the Grange and became a constant visitor. Once Freddy established that there was no danger to his precious Miss Shauna, he was very willing to fall under Kit's easy charm, and the two became fast friends. The twins found they, too, rather enjoyed the newcomer, for he was certainly lively.

Two days had passed since Damien had left for London, and Shauna would have been devastatingly heartsick had she not both Kit and Freddy to pick up her spirits. Kit knew her, though, very well, and he was not fooled by her false air of merriness. They were sitting on the stone bench by the duck pond watching the twins feed the ducks when he asked, suddenly serious, "What is it, girl? Why so blue-deviled?"

"Not so," she answered quickly, too quickly.

"This is me you are talking to, my child," he returned on a superior note. "Can't fool me."

"Child indeed!" She attempted to divert the subject.

"I have eight months on you and a vast deal more experience; besides, *I* am a man"—he put up his hand to halt the tirade he could see she was about to let loose on him—"a superior creature, my dear, while you are but a woman."

His teasing was mitigated with a brotherly kiss dropped on her nose. "Now, what has you so low?"

"Naught," she answered quietly. She had always confided in Kit. She had told him about her first kiss and every kiss after that, much to his jibes and lectures. She had told him about every scrape and lark she had ever kicked up, including all her notorious adventures in London. She had never held back, and yet she found she now could not speak about Damien.

"Indeed?" He was taken aback and slightly hurt by her reticence.

"It is just . . . so very difficult to speak about. . . ." She allowed the sentence to trail off. Something kept her silent. She could not say what; she only knew she couldn't speak about her feelings for Damien, have those feelings ridiculed by Kit in his usual fashion. She was no longer larking.

"Is it?" He prompted her to go on. "Try, one word at a time. One sentence following another. It often works."

"I . . . I can't. . . ." Shauna found she was blushing furiously.

"Damnation, boy!" Kit was on his feet and rushing towards the pond. "Don't go on those rocks!"

Too late. Felix's foot had already slipped on the slimy surface, causing him to do a split between two rocks. He released a yell of some proportions, lost his balance, and went bodily into the pond.

There was a great deal of commotion that ensued because of this, and for some hours afterwards Felix's escapade was the butt of much joking. Shauna's blues were set aside for a time, but only for a time.

The next morning brought Kit boldly into the breakfast parlor. He was heartily greeted by all and told to join them at the table. He declined, advising them that he had been up for hours, breakfasted earlier, and was now ready for a tour of Bromley.

Freddy jumped up immediately. He had taken on a new sense of responsibility, and the notion of giving Kit—whom he now recognized as a top sawyer Corinthian—a tour of his lands was most exciting.

"Right you are!" said Freddy, going toward the doors.

Shauna laughed and waved them off. Her depression once again descended, but there was no time for that. She had the twins and their lessons to attend to for the remainder of the morning, and though she did this, it was not with her usual enthusiasm.

It was nearly noon. The twins were in the dining room munching on the cold collation that had been prepared for them and requesting to go afterwards to see "mama cat's kittens." Shauna smiled indulgently and agreed to it when the dining room door opened and both Kit and Freddy strode inside.

"Well," laughed Shauna, "don't you both look, er . . . healthy." She eyed them up and down, for both young men looked a bit dishevelled.

"We raced, you see," explained Freddy, going to the sideboard for a plate.

"Did you?" Shauna sensed there was more to this story.

"For the . . . love of a woman," put in Kit with a hand to his heart.

"Never say so," laughed Shauna.

"Indeed. Said she would have the winner, and she did!" chuckled Kit.

Freddy was blushing, and Shauna turned inquiring eyes. "And there, Freddy . . . you swore me love to your last breath or some such nonsense. Men are fickle beings."

"Yes, well, it wasn't my fault and I didn't win her. Kit did."

She turned to Kit. "Et tu, Brute?"

"No, no. I won her, but I gave her to Freddy." He was grinning broadly. "Ain't in the petticoat line meself, as you

112

well know. Besides, her peasant beauty wasn't in my style. Too buxom for me.''

"Freddy?" Shauna's brow was up. "What did you do, you dreadful boy?"

"One doesn't kiss and tell," stuck in Kit.

Freddy threatened him with a fork, and much jesting followed, so that no one noticed as a tall, striking man entered the dining room to survey this scene.

Felix was the first to exclaim and go forward. "Damien! Damien!"

Shauna nearly gasped. She turned round and found his blue eyes, and she did stop breathing for a moment.

Kit looked at this Lord Drummond and to himself went, Well, well . . . what the deuce is this? for he recognized his lordship at once. It did not occur to him that Drummond and the Bromleys were related. How Drummond had found Shauna he could not guess, but it would now appear that he would have to protect her from him. He stepped forward and went to Shauna's side.

Damien picked up Felix, put him down, patted his head, and then took up Francine to drop a kiss on her nose. Having put them down, his eyes once more found Shauna's gray ones and he felt his world shaken beneath his feet. That one woman could have such an effect on him was unthinkable.

"Welcome home, my lord," Shauna said softly, and her lashes brushed her cheek.

Welcome home? Kit looked from Shauna to Damien. What does she mean, welcome home? Why did the twins greet him so warmly? What was going on?

"Thank you," he answered just as softly.

"Damien . . . we are going to see mama cat's kittens. Want to come?" Francine pulled on his jacket sleeve.

"You two go on. . . . Maybe I'll join you later," he answered, and looked toward Kit. Here was an extremely personable young man. Who was he? What was he doing standing so close to Shauna? His brow went up.

Shauna's manners returned and she interjected quickly, "Oh, Kit, I am sorry. This is Lord Damien Drummond. He is the Bromleys' brother." She turned to Kit. "My very dear friend, Lord Christopher Dartford."

Kit was doing some fast thinking. Here was Lord Drummond. Didn't Shauna realize? No, of course not. She had run away without even knowing who it was she was supposed to marry. Hell! What a tangle. What to do? He stood speechless for a split second before he was able to go through with the usual amenities. However, with his habitual jolly charm he greeted Damien.

Lord Drummond experienced a severe pang of jealousy, so very severe, in fact, that he was unable to look at Kit without gritting his teeth. What the devil did she mean, her "very dear friend"? What was this young scamp doing in his home? Did Dartford think he could have her? Was that why he was here? She seemed to like Dartford. Damn, look at the way she smiled at the lad! Damn. This jealousy resulted in a black mood descending over him, and he was scarcely civil to young Dartford. Instead he went to Freddy, patted his shoulder, and said he would only be a few moments, for he meant to go look in on the twins and the kittens. With a glare at Shauna, he left the room.

She peeped, for it dawned on her that he was actually jealous.

"Do you think that look was meant for me?" she asked of Freddy. "Perhaps he thinks I should be overseeing this project?"

"Go on then, Shauna. Kit and I will sit a bit longer over our lunch. No doubt he will want to know everything the twins have been up to while he was away. I wouldn't mention the pond incident while he is in one of his moods, though."

Shauna laughed. "I have a sound mind, my dear." She started out of the room.

Kit found his voice. "Shauna. . . ?" Then he stopped himself. He couldn't very well blurt out in front of Freddy that Drummond was the man she had run away from, now could he? Freddy knew now that Shauna was in hiding from her family, but he didn't know the whole. Better keep it till later.

"Yes, Kit?"

"Naught. Go on . . . go on."

She puzzled up, but anxious to go to Drummond, she did not pursue the matter. "Don't go without seeing me, Kit." She put up a finger.

"Wouldn't dream of loping off without taking my leave of you, brat." He smiled at her and then applied himself to his food.

Kit's attitude haunted her for a few minutes. She knew him very well, and there was something on his mind. In fact, she was fairly certain it had to do with Damien. This, however, was momentarily forgotten as she reached the barn. Damien turned, and their eyes met.

"Aren't they precious?" she asked softly.

"Hardly," he answered on a chuckle, and moved toward her. "Though they might be in a few days. The twins are fascinated with them. Francine thinks them 'utterly divine.' "

Shauna laughed. "Do you know, my lord, a notion has occurred to me . . . that I should like to discuss with you."

"Certainly." He fell in step with her and they moved away from the children and the barn's enclosure.

"I think it would do the twins a great deal of good to spend some time in London. There is much to be learned in town . . . that is important to their education." She could not help looking into his eyes, so very intensely blue.

He wanted to catch her up, hold her, kiss her. His hands clasped one another at his back as he walked beside her, but he found himself devouring her with his eyes. "An interesting proposition. I shall consider it."

"Thank you." She stopped. She felt awkward. There was nothing else she found herself able to say, so she started off.

He stopped her. "Is that all?"

She smiled. "Should there be more?"

"How did you go on while I was gone?" He answered her question with one of his own.

She laughed, "We managed . . ."

"In spite of Felix?" he prompted.

Her eyes flashed. "You know, then?"

He chuckled, "Felix told me about his adventure. He enjoyed it immensely."

"Oh, Damien, I wish you could have seen his face before and after. It was so comical. But he was such a good sport and took a great deal of ribbing from Freddy and Kit."

"Ah, I was forgetting Kit." Damien stopped and looked at her. "An old flame come to visit?"

"An old friend." She looked away.

Kit was coming towards them. He watched their exchange and was hit with a sudden suspicion. "Whew, now what is this?" he asked no one in particular.

"Hallo!" he called out to let them know he was approaching.

Shauna smiled at him. "Oh no, never say you are leaving?"

"No choice. Time ran away with me. Freddy has to hit his books, and I am promised to friends in Southampton. Drop in on you tomorrow, sweetheart." He nodded at Damien and went after his horse. This was something he had to think about. Just what would Shauna say when she found out she was governess to the brother and sister of the man she had run away from? What would Damien say when he discovered Shauna's true identity? Lord, what a muddle! *He had to think.*

Chapter Nineteen

True to his word, Kit arrived the next morning in time to join the Bromleys at breakfast. He piled his dish high with food and kept a lively banter going with both Freddy and Shauna. During this time he watched Damien discreetly. When Damien noticed this, he drew his own conclusions.

So, thought Damien, this scamp is appraising me as a rival. He is here for Shauna and no doubt means to take her back with him. Look at him, ingratiating himself with Freddy and the twins. Why, they all dote on the fellow. This, he decided, was insufferable. Damien found himself unable to control his emotions, though he did control his tongue. His bad mood could be detected by the curtness of his tone and the touch of a sneer about his lips.

Shauna watched him, and when he glanced her way, she looked flirtatiously at him. He could not help but grin at her. She always managed to wring a smile out of him, even when he was determined to do otherwise. Soon afterwards she excused herself and the twins, advising the gentlemen that they were off to the schoolroom to do lessons. Felix grumbled and Francine moaned that it was such a lovely day, too lovely to be stuck indoors, but Shauna merely smiled and ushered them along.

"She is good with them," remarked Kit. "Absurd chit."

"What is that you say?" Damien rounded on him. What the devil did this scamp mean talking about her in that familiar way?

"Well"—Kit had to cover his slip—"What I meant was that, well, Shauna and I have been friends ever since we started toddling about, you see . . . and I have never before realized how capable she is with children."

"Really?" returned Damien frostily. "Miss Shauna is more capable than most women in her position."

"Right. Well . . ." said Kit, getting to his feet, "I think I'll go join them in the schoolroom and see her in action."

"What?" Damien nearly shrieked.

"Oh, I know the way," replied Kit, already out the door.

Freddy watched this exchange with keen interest. He could see that his brother objected to Kit.

"Damn his impudence!" snapped Damien, throwing his napkin on the table and getting to his feet.

"Oh, never mind. He is the best of good fellows, Damien. Really . . . you have to give him a chance."

"A chance? A chance to do what? Take Shauna off, just when the twins were doing so well?"

"Is that what you think?" scoffed Freddy. " 'Cause he won't. Can't. Tried, and Shauna wouldn't go."

"What?" shrieked his lordship again. "How do you know?"

"I was there, the first day he arrived. Came here to take her back with him. She wouldn't go . . . said the twins needed her. So you needn't worry. Said she wouldn't go till the twins were able to get on without her."

His lordship paced. So it was true. This—this Dartford came to steal Shauna. He knew it. . . . Any man would come after her . . . take her if he could. She might go. After all, Dartford was young, perhaps foolish enough to even offer marriage. That was it; she was holding out for marriage, and this Dartford . . . by God, no doubt he

118

would end in offering it, and then Shauna . . . Shauna would be lost to him! With this notion burning in his brain he made his way to the stairs with every intention of joining the party in the schoolroom.

The twins were quietly working on a writing assignment when Kit appeared and cocked a brow, indicating to Shauna that he wanted private speech with her. She went with him into the hall and whispered, "What is it, Kit?"

"Shauna . . . we have to talk. There is something you have to know. . . ."

"Now?" She was surprised.

"Obviously not now . . . but soon . . . Shauna . . . there is something I must tell you, for if I don't, I think you might kill me, and probably rightly so."

"Kit. . . ?" She put her hands on his arms. "What is the matter? What are you talking about?"

The sound of approaching footsteps brought both their heads round. They looked guilty, not because of anything other than being caught telling secrets, but their startled, guilty expressions sent Damien's already frazzled temper into the boughs.

"Do I intrude?" he asked dryly.

"Not at all," Shauna returned hurriedly, perhaps too sharply. "Kit was just taking his leave of me. Weren't you, my lord?"

"Ay . . . ay . . . till later then." He started down the hallway, but he felt incomplete, and his steps were precise, slow.

Shauna watched him and then said, "Excuse me, my lord . . . I just remembered something I want to tell Lord Dartford before he leaves." She rushed after Kit and stopped him at the head of the stairs to whisper, "I shall meet you at the spinney near your inn at five o'clock."

"Right," he answered, pleased enough with this.

Shauna turned and realized that Damien was staring at

her in a hard, strange manner. She very nearly gulped. Such power he had over her senses. She found it difficult to meet his eyes, but managed the feat with a half-smile. "You wanted to see me, my lord?"

"Indeed. I thought I did," he answered coldly. "However, I find that you are busy, and whatever I wanted . . . no longer seems important." He turned away from her and started off.

"My lord. . . ?" she called after him.

He stopped, but his mouth was set and his posture frosty. "Yes?"

"Nothing," she answered, and went into the schoolroom. This was ridiculous. What was wrong with him? He was the one making improper propositions to the governess of his family. He was the one who thought a governess beneath his station, not high enough in the instep to make his wife. He was the one who took off for London without a word. . . . And he was the one who commanded all her thoughts, all her feelings.

Kit was pacing. It was already five minutes past five o'clock, and Shauna was nowhere to be seen. However, just as he was starting to get nervous, he saw her walking her horse on foot through the sparsely wooded field, and he went toward her. "Well, 'tis about time, madcap!"

"I got here as fast as I could. Damien seemed to be hanging about the stables. I had the devil of a time trying to get away without his seeing me."

"What difference does it make whether he sees you leave or not? For pity's sake, Shauna, you are Miss Elton of Elton House, not a governess and not a Corbett!"

"Oh, Kit, you don't understand. . . ." she started to whine.

"I don't understand? Dunce, it's you who has lost your reason. Look, m'girl, do you know who Drummond is?"

"What kind of a stupid question is that?" returned Shauna, incensed with him now.

"No, of course you do not. You didn't take the time to find out who your mama matched you with. Well, let me tell you, had you known, you would not have run away!"

"Oh, really? What makes you so cocksure, you wretched boy?"

"I ain't blind. Saw the way you looked at him," Kit replied pugnaciously.

"I believe you are mad," answered Shauna to this. "Indeed, the poor lad is mad. It's all this fresh country air. . . . It has gone to his head."

"Stupid little madcap!" he laughed, and then took her shoulders. "It's Drummond. Don't you see? . . . It's Drummond."

"What is Drummond? What are you trying to tell me?"

"You are engaged to marry Drummond. He goes off to London to check on his intended bride . . . who is above-stairs with a quinsy, then he comes to Bromley and makes eyes at you. It is actually very funny when you think about it."

Shauna was struck, and it was not with amusement. Her gray eyes were open wide, and she was clutching Kit's sleeve. "What are you trying to tell me? Damien . . . Damien offered for me? Why . . . but why . . . " Then dawning, "Of course . . . it all makes sense. That night he was drunk . . . had to meet his fiancée the next morning—me! Oh my word . . . I am engaged to Damien!"

Kit frowned. "Why don't you look happy? Had a notion you might like the idea . . . seem to like Drummond. He seems to have a tendre in your direction. All seems right and tight!"

"Well, it is not! He won't like that I have deceived him. If I honor the engagement, he will never know if I am marrying him to meet my commitment as an Elton or if I

121

am marrying him for love, and Kit . . . I want him to know it is for love. Oh, Kit . . . I must leave for London . . . right away. I must quarrel with him and get myself dismissed. . . . And the twins . . . I shall have to explain to them.''

"Hmmm. Problem there; they are rather fond of you.''

"Freddy shall take care of them. I will return in a week with a presentable governess . . . just the sort they should have, and I shall select her myself. Kit . . .''

"Yes?'' He looked at her warily.

"You must be ready to escort me back to London to-night. Can you hire a post chaise for the trip? I don't want anyone to see me riding into London. I have to do this quietly.''

"Done. Be back here at seven, and off we'll go,'' he answered her promptly. "I've had a chaise in waiting ever since I found you.''

She threw her arms round his neck and planted a kiss on his cheek. "I will be back promptly at seven. . . .'' So saying, she turned and made for the woodland trail.

Shauna didn't get very far. Damien sat his horse in the middle of the narrow trail. She saw him and pulled up on her reins, for she had been gently cantering her horse. She found herself breathing irregularly and wondered what he was doing there looking so oddly at her. "Damien . . . my lord, how . . . nice . . .'' she said lamely.

"Is it? . . . Nice, I mean?'' he asked her dryly.

"Well, of course; finding myself in your company is always pleasant.''

"Fine; shall I escort you home then?'' he asked blandly.

She shot an inquiring glance his way but could read nothing from his cold expression. "Thank you.''

"Did you have a, er . . . pleasant visit with your friend Dartford?'' he asked almost too casually.

"What makes you think I was visiting Kit?" she returned, her chin starting up.

"Weren't you?"

"As a matter of fact, yes, I was."

"I can't say I approve of such behavior in the governess of my brother and sister," he said on a hard note.

"No, of course not. I understand perfectly. You reserve the right to take favors from your employees!" She said this with calculation. She wanted him angry. She needed to quarrel with him so that she might be able to leave him in anger.

He reached out to stop her horse, for she was cantering away from him and they were almost near the Bromley drive. "Hold there, sweetheart!" He did in fact rein in her animal.

"Stop that!" she snapped. "I don't like being manhandled."

"Then don't make sharp remarks and then take off. Expect to get as good as you give . . . " So saying, he slipped his arm round her waist and drew her to him for a kiss. Their lips barely met when Shauna's horse fidgeted away.

She wanted to giggle but rode instead toward the barn. Damien rode after her, but this time he made no attempt to stop her. When they reached the stables he quickly called the groom to take both their horses, and followed as Shauna started for the house.

"Shauna . . . wait," he called after her. "I should like ten minutes of your time."

She turned. "Of course, my lord."

He caught up to her and drew her toward a stone bench lining a bluestone path, and there made her sit beside him. "Shauna . . . you must know how I feel about you. . . . "

"Must I?" she returned, her brow up. "Kit tells me that you are engaged to marry Lady Elton's stepdaughter."

He drew himself up. "That is true, but . . . Shauna . . . I want you . . . and I think you want me."

"What makes you think so, my lord?"

"Is it that puppy, Dartford, then?" He had drawn himself up ramrod straight.

She relented, "No . . . it is you; it has been you from the first moment you kissed me that night I was running away . . . but I won't be your mistress!" So saying, she got to her feet and ran, praying he would not follow.

She was right. He did not, could not. What could he say? He adored her, wanted her . . . certes, he loved her! What could he do? He was engaged to marry the Elton chit, and until he was free of that entanglement, he could not make her any promises. Forgotten was the fact that she was a governess, beneath his station. She was Shauna, queen of his heart, and he wanted her.

Chapter Twenty

"Freddy!" Shauna called to him in the library. "Conference, quickly . . . in the schoolroom." She didn't wait for him to ask her any questions but ran to the stairs and nearly took them two at a time. Speed. It was all-important that she be gone before Damien confronted her again. She wouldn't bother packing. Faith, it would be good to have her entire wardrobe at her disposal again.

She found the twins playing at a board game in Francine's room and ushered them to the schoolroom. "We need to talk. Come."

They sensed something important was afoot and followed her in hushed silence. Freddy met them as they entered, and Shauna closed the door. "Sit . . . all of you . . ."

Freddy looked round for something, but other than a footstool, he could find nothing his size. "Can't," he answered her simply.

She would have giggled had she time; instead she restrained herself and said, "I have to go . . . tonight. . . ." She put up her hands as they started to object, but then Francine was throwing herself at her and hugging her thighs. "No, Miss Shauna . . . you can't!"

"Hush, love. I shan't be gone long . . . a week, two at the most . . . but I must run, and tonight. There is something . . . personal that I must attend to in London. Lord Dartford has offered to escort me. I can't tell you more, but I am asking you to trust me and believe me. . . . I shall make everything alright."

"No, no, no," cried Francine.

"Stuff it!" ordered Felix. "Didn't you hear Miss Shauna? She will be back. She promised."

"That's a brave lad. You trust me. . . ." She took Francine's chin. "And you?"

"I . . . I . . . trust . . . you," sobbed Francine.

Shauna dropped a kiss on her nose. "I shall be back. There isn't a soul alive that could stop me from coming back, but you promise me not to tell Damien. I don't want him to know that I have promised to come back. Understood?"

"A secret then?" Felix liked secrets.

"A secret," smiled Shauna.

Freddy had been silent, thoughtfully silent, but he drew himself up and said, "You can rely on me, Miss Shauna. I shall look after the twins until you return, and I am pledged to your secret."

"I know, Freddy, and I am relying on you."

"You will come back and be our governess forever," said Francine.

"No, love. I will come back . . . but not as your governess." She put a finger to Francine's trembling lips. "You and Felix have made such a wonderful push in the right direction. What you both need now is someone who can really teach you what you need to learn, what you need to know before you go off to school in a few years. Trust me, I'll bring you that special someone, and you will like her as much as you like me."

"No, never, never!" Francine cried in loyal accents.

"Never mind. I do promise to come back, but it is our secret. Remember, you must not tell Damien that I am returning. Now, I must run." She kissed Francine and

126

then Felix. "Trust me, darlings, do, for you may, and I shan't let you down in this."

Shauna moved to Freddy. "Lessons, Freddy. Make them do their letters, speak to them in French, take them on outings, and by the time I get back, it will nearly be time for you to leave for Eton."

He laughed, "Shauna . . . I . . . we—we shall miss you."

She touched his cheek. "And I you . . . all of you. Now I am off. Remember, when Damien asks, you may tell him I have left him a letter on my mantelshelf. It is all the explanation I mean to give him."

So saying, she went off to pen a letter to his lordship. After some hurried scribbling and wasted paper, she came up with:

My Lord Drummond, _

I have enjoyed my stay at Bromley. I adore the twins, and my time with them is something that is very precious to me. However, it is apparent that I cannot remain under the same roof with you, for reasons we both understand.

Forgive me. I have made an explanation to the twins and to Freddy, and I shall send you an exceptional woman to take my place. Yes, I do know someone who would be perfect for the position.

Again, forgive me, but it seems that running away from things I cannot handle is something I am falling into the habit of doing. Cowardly but expedient.

Fondly,
Shauna

This done, she put the hood of her cloak over her thick silk waves of black hair and quietly left the house. It would take her a good twenty minutes to walk the distance to Kit, but she was on time. Everything seemed to be in order, and if so, why did she feel so very heartsick? This was the answer, wasn't it? Faith, let it be the answer!

Damien had a fitful night. When he dozed it was to find himself enmeshed in the sort of nightmares that left him in a cold sweat. Each time he would wake with Shauna's name on his lips. He would toss and turn, sit up, walk about, throw himself on his mattress, and wonder what the devil he was going to do about this problem. It certainly was a problem.

He dressed himself, snapped at his valet, pushed away the morning tray of hot chocolate, and made his way downstairs. There he looked in at the breakfast room to find a gloomy threesome. The twins and Freddy were inside, but there was no sign of Shauna.

"Where is your governess?" he asked the twins.

"Gone," said Francine sadly.

"Gone? What do you mean gone?" Damien's blue eyes snapped to attention.

"She left last night," added Freddy. "Said she couldn't stay."

"What the bloody hell are you talking about? Why couldn't she stay? Where would she go?"

"Said Freddy was to give us our lessons until she sent us a new governess," put in Felix. "But we don't want another governess; we want Miss Shauna."

"How could she go . . . without even an explanation to me?" Damien said out loud, for it gnawed him that he knew why she left.

"Left you a letter on her mantelshelf," said Freddy, watching his brother's distress with keen interest. This was most enlightening. He had never seen his brother quite this frazzled over anything.

"Did she, by God!" With which Damien wheeled round and made for the stairs.

When he found the letter he hesitated before opening it.

Something inside of him trembled. Why would she go? Where did she go? Had she gone with that young puppy, Dartford? Certes, he couldn't bear it. . . .

The last line of Shauna's letter he read over and over again. "Cowardly but expedient." He had caused this to happen. She had been good for the twins, and he had forced her to run away. What choice did she have when he had made it impossible for her to stay? Shauna . . .

Where could she have gone? He must find her. Dartford. Perhaps Dartford would know. He pulled at the bell-rope and ordered his horse to be tacked up and brought to the front of the house. He would go and see Dartford!

Damien rode to the inn at a heady pace. It was too late, of course, to stop Shauna from going—she was gone, he knew that—but he needed the run. He handed his horse to a livery boy and commanded him to walk his animal down while he went within to see Mr. Regis.

Regis was a stout and jolly man. He had long prospered at his Red Bull Tavern and was proud of his establishment. He was polishing his dark oak bar counter when he looked up to find a tall, arresting figure of a man, and he smiled a welcome. Lord Drummond was well known and liked by most of the locals.

"Good morning to ye, my lord," Regis greeted and put down his cloth. He could see that Drummond wanted a word with him.

"And to you, Regis," his lordship nodded, but was too impatient to waste time on the usual amenities. "Regis, tell me, is young Dartford upstairs?"

"No, my lord. He left us last evening," said Regis, frowning, for he could see that Drummond was greatly perturbed by this piece of information.

"Last evening? Did he . . . do you know if he had anyone with him when he left here?"

"Couldn't say . . . but he did hire a post chaise . . .

hitched that fine piece of horseflesh of his to the boot, and off he went."

"Did he mention where he intended to go?"

"London . . . ay, that's it. Thanked me, paid his fare, and said he was off for London."

"London! Well, by God, we shall see!" returned Damien, too hot at hand to think how he sounded.

Regis watched him stride out of the inn and rubbed his chin. What was this now? Then he shook his head and went about his business. There was no sense in what the quality was forever after. Strange lot, the aristocracy, forever on some chase or other!

Chapter Twenty-one

Lady Elton came rushing into the parlor. She had been out, and, upon her return was informed by Jarves, the Elton butler, that all was right with the world once more—Miss Shauna was home!

She saw Shauna, now ensconced in one of her pretty morning gowns of pale green, sipping tea with Kit, who was recounting a lively anecdote for her to alleviate her tension.

"There you are! Oh, my darling love . . ." Lady Elton nearly wept as she went forward to meet Shauna, who was rushing to her.

They embraced for a full minute before Lady Elton set her aside and advised her, "You are the most wicked, dreadful, horridest, unfeeling brat alive, and I am heartily glad you are home safe and sound."

"Oh, Mama . . . I am sorry, truly; I did not mean to make you weep, but I could not, will not marry a stranger."

"No, no, of course you shall not. It is just that Drummond . . . well, I rather think him perfect for you."

"So he is," peeped Shauna.

"So he is?" Lady Elton turned to Kit for help.

"There, isn't that a female for you!" grinned Kit.

131

"Well, I must be going. I'll drop by again tomorrow, my girl, for tonight I mean to sleep."

"Of all the paltry things . . . ." Shauna laughed. "You said you would have dinner with us."

"Can't," he answered laconically.

"Why not?" she asked, curious but wary.

"Don't want to," he returned glibly, and made for the door in time to duck the throw pillow that came hurtling at his head.

He was gone, and Shauna found herself facing her mother alone. She drew breath and said, "Come then, Mama, we shall have a nice long chat and then we shall send for Mrs. Epsom."

"Mrs. Epsom?" Lady Elton was diverted into asking, though silently she chastised herself for her lapse.

"Indeed, I find that I can now solve an earlier dilemma with a new one. Put them together and both end happily."

"My dear . . . what are you talking about?" Lady Elton's eyes opened wide and she knew that once more Shauna was weaving yet another adventure.

"Remember poor Mrs. Epsom? She is Lady Hatley's poverty-stricken cousin."

"Yes, but—"

"Well, I could not help but pity her, for she is a darling woman with the best of dispositions, and Lady Hatley uses her abominably. What she needs is a genteel position . . . and I have one for her."

"Do you? But . . . could we, if you will, first discuss where the deuce you have been this last month?" Lady Elton was moved to shout.

"I was coming to that, Mama . . . and, dearest, thank you. What did I have that kept me abed for so long?"

"The measles, a quinsy . . . it depended on who was calling," Lady Elton sighed to answer. "The servants adore you. . . . They kept your secret under lock and key. You must thank them all."

"So I shall. . . . Oh, Mama, you should have told me I was engaged to marry Lord Drummond." There was a twinkle in her gray eyes.

Lady Elton sat up hopefully. "But you never gave me the opportunity, you awful girl."

"Well, I shall do so now. . . . Why do you think he offered for me? He had never before set eyes on me."

"I believe he wanted a mother for his young brother and sister, and perhaps he thought it was time he started a family of his own . . . why?"

"Why, because I have decided to have him. . . . But, Mama, I think he may arrive here soon to cry off. . . . You know, we must not allow him to do so."

"Shauna, I may strangle you. What has happened? Where have you been, and why have you suddenly decided to have Drummond?"

"Oh, Mama . . . I will start at the beginning. . . . Here, relax . . . 'tis a long story."

Chapter Twenty-two

Damien discovered that Dartford had lodgings in Kensington Square. He had been on the road for four hours. He was dusty, he was tired, and he was hungry, but before he attended to his bodily needs, he would see Kit!

As the door to Kit's lodgings opened, Damien felt a certain fear grip his heart. What if she was already under Dartford's protection? What if she was already Dartford's mistress? Lost to him. . . ? No. This was unthinkable. Dartford's man appeared at the door, and Drummond was advised that his lordship had set out for his club, White's.

Damien could have killed. He restrained himself, thanked the butler, and hurried down the steps to the urchin holding his horse. He flipped the child a coin, jumped nimbly into the saddle, and made his way to his own town house in Grovsnor. If Kit was at his club, then of course Shauna was not with him. He would bathe, change, have a bite to eat, and go to Dartford's lodgings later in the day. That Dartford had taken Shauna to London, he was fairly certain; however, he was also certain she was safely being housed and not yet touched. He felt confident of this because he knew Shauna. There was still time. He would find her, and damn, when he did . . . he would make her his own, at any cost!

* * *

Kit entered his lodgings and was given Damien's calling card. His brow went up. "Do you mean to tell me Lord Drummond was here? Asking for me, was he?" He scarcely had his answer when the knocker sounded and his man left him to open the front door. Kit turned to see who it was and was surprised to find Damien striding into the hall.

"Dartford"—this from Damien—"may I have private speech with you?"

"Zounds, man . . . you look the very devil! What is wrong with you?" Kit was amusing himself, for indeed, Damien looked nearly sick with jealousy. He took pity and turned to lead the way to the study. He opened the door, allowed Damien to enter, and then followed, closing the door at his back and saying, "Can I pour you some brandy?"

"No, but you can give me some straight answers."

"Can I?"

"Dartford, I am aware that you left with Shauna . . . and I am here to bring her back to Bromley."

"Are you?" Kit smiled kindly. "She does not wish to go back at this time."

"What does she wish? To remain in London . . . with you?"

"Not precisely." Kit was evasive.

"Dartford . . . look . . . I . . . I care for her . . . a great deal. When she left it was because I led her to believe that . . . that I was only interested in making her my mistress. . . ."

"Aren't you?"

"Yes, no . . . I was then . . . but now . . ."

"My Lord Drummond. *I* care for Shauna, and you cannot make her anything else while you are engaged to marry Miss Elton, who is also a friend of mine!"

Damien was silenced a moment and then he sighed, "I was forgetting that . . . Never mind it, I intend to break that off. The arrangement was never completed, the banns never posted, the settlement never signed. Miss Elton has been ill for some weeks, and we were never . . . introduced.''

"Good God! You were going to marry a woman you had never met?''

"Well . . . yes, but . . .'' Damien shook his head. "Never mind that. Only tell me where I might find Shauna. I have to speak to her.''

"I will, but only after you have settled your affairs with Miss Elton,'' Kit said gently. Egad, but this was one famous adventure.

"At this hour?'' Damien was irritated and unused to being handled. He sensed that somehow he was being manipulated, and eyed Kit suspiciously. "I don't know that Lady Elton will see me.''

"It is Miss Elton you have to see.''

"Yes, but she is ill. . . .''

"No longer,'' answered Kit.

"Devil you say! How do you happen to know?'' Damien was now studying Kit thoughtfully. Something was very odd about all of this, though he couldn't put a finger on it.

"Because I paid her a morning visit . . . and she was quite well.''

"Right then. As you say . . . I will tidy up my affairs but, Dartford, when I return . . . no more games. I will have Shauna's direction.''

"As you say . . . after you visit Miss Elton, there should be no more games,'' replied Kit.

Shauna pushed away her tea and cake, for she felt restless. She took a tour of the room, swishing the skirts of her pretty day gown of white muslin round her provocative figure. She played with a stray hair of black silk at her ear and looked up as her butler announced, "Lord Damien Drummond." She caught her breath and waited.

Damien stopped short. His hat was already off; he dropped it and left it where it fell. He stuttered her name and took a step forward and then stopped. "Shauna . . . how . . . what are you, I don't understand. . . ?"

"No, of course you don't. What are you doing here, my lord?" Shauna attempted sangfroid, but her heart was beating wildly.

"I came here to see Miss Elton . . . to . . . to explain that I can't marry her. . . . Shauna . . . are you related to Miss Elton?"

"Can't marry her?" Shauna clucked. "Just when I was getting used to the notion."

He went to her then and took up her shoulders. "What is going on here? Shauna, explain."

"What shall I explain? That I love you, my lord?"

He kissed her then, groaned and set her aside. "Shauna, you ran away from me . . . came here. . . ."

"You wanted me to be your mistress. . . . You were getting married, and wanted a piece of muslin on the side. I couldn't be that fancy piece. . . ." she answered softly.

"I don't want you to be a fancy piece. I love you, Shauna, love you. I want you to be my wife. . . ." Something nagged at him. "What do you mean you were getting used to the idea of my marrying Miss Elton?"

"When my stepmama told me she had chosen a husband for me, I didn't even wait to hear his name. . . . I just took off . . . in the middle of the night . . . and there you were. . . ."

Dawning! He took her shoulders again. "Shauna!"

"Exactly. Then Kit came and told me who you were, and I thought I would like to be married to you, so I came back to be Miss Elton again, you see, and now here you are breaking off our engagement." She shook her head. "That is not very nice."

"Shauna!" he called, and started to laugh, for he was a man in love, a man relieved, but then he remembered the offenses committed against him. "Why didn't you just tell me. . . ?"

"Thought you might be moved to passion if you thought I had run off with Kit. Wanted you moved to passion."

"You miserable female!" he said, and kissed her long and tenderly. When he allowed her air, he said, "And the twins; what is to be done for the twins?"

"I have that settled all right and tight. . . . What I want to know, my lord—is ¯. . . our marriage . . . off . . . or on?"

He gave her his answer with action, sweet, ardent, and left her with no doubts . . . no doubts whatsoever.